OPERATION: DOUBLE-CROSS

by

CHARLES NUETZEL

WRITING AS "GEORGE FREDRICS"

The Borgo Press
An Imprint of Wildside Press

MMVII

CONTENTS

INTRODUCTION

This book was written during a time when the world was, after World War II, locked in a Cold War struggle between the superpowers: the USA and USSR. This radically changed under President Reagan. In 1989 the Berlin Wall was torn down and the Soviet Union was shattered for good.

But during this period the world was held in a strange kind of balance, one that is now restructured under the terrible threat of a new kind of warfare. Huge armies don't need to face one another. Today a war can rage by the simple use of madmen willing to blow themselves up for the promise of a heavenly reward—or merely the belief that their families will profit by such violent acts. They see themselves as heroes! And since history is always written by the winners, they may ultimately be considered either that—or monstrous fools.

The world religions all seek answers, and offer moral lessons; they all are powerful forces that have shaped civilizations.

Islam is as spiritually uplifting to its faithful as the Christianity is to its believers. Both major religions are based on the same historical elements that formed early Judaism. All are a result of very ancient teachings handed down from generation to generation. And each has had its own Prophets that inspired the major religious movements that are now in a hostile state of anguished conflict.

Enough to say; without in any way taking sides, these power-blocks are pretty much after the same limited resources the planet offers us all.

History is filled with claims of Religious Ultimate Answers driving nations and empires into violent conflict. Are we, today, in any better position? Rome fell, as did the ancient lands of Mesopotamia. National boundaries fluctuate to satisfy the needs of their populations, and they are endlessly redrawn.

So we come to today's nightmare of horrors, conflicts between religiously dedicated power blocks. Death comes fast and easy, life ebbs and flows like ocean waves. And the soldier or patriot or terrorist will give up their lives in this endless struggle for world dominance.

The world of terrorists since 9/11 has changed how we all live, and has effected everything in this new century. And in this book, I've managed to update the setting and time-frame of the original novel to fit into this twenty-first-century reality.

—CHARLES NUETZEL
Thousand Oaks, California
August 2006

CHAPTER ONE

It was a top secret meeting set in the heart of a large building coded x. The room was battered by time, a small desk in the center had worn edges, marred with age. The lighting was subdued, the atmosphere edging on the melodramatic.

The man sitting behind the desk was tall and thin, his actions nervous; his eyes, harsh serious lines. He was a man dedicated to his job, dedicated to his cause—to his nation. His code name was Agent Baker. He was talking to the man opposite him who sat quietly, speaking only when necessary. This man was known as Agent Green.

Baker said: "I thought you'd like to know Hern Industries are involved, this time."

Green's face tightened, his eyes narrowed and the cigar paused in mid-air, inches from waiting lips. Otherwise he revealed no emotions of what was going on in his mind.

"I'm concerning that there's a terrorist connection involved this time. And a man named Fats Delano has an importing contract with a go-between outfit called Renton, Inc. We just discovered this the other day. He's shipping heroin. But his connections

7

go into the East, into Iran, and Iraq and Al-Qaida… and there's the danger. And especially after the London bombings. Things are getting very iffy."

Baker paused a moment and then continued: "I understand this contract means a lot to Hern Industries. And I know what it means to you if that company became involved in some international scandal. That's why I'm offering you this assignment. You're to break up this connection—the headquarters are in the South Pacific. At least cripple it, don't let things go through on this one."

Green nodded, saying nothing. His face displayed no emotion.

"I also understand Greg Hern is going to Temming Island to work out a merger with John Judson."

"So I'm told," Green smiled. It was the first sign of humor to move the muscles of the man's handsome features.

"That's another reason I'm giving you this one. Nose around Temming Island. See if you can find any connection between Fats Delano and Judson or Bedford. There's a connection somewhere. Break it!"

The conversation continued, filling in details of the new assignment. Agent Green finally stood and shook hands.

"Good luck. Just remember we can't help you if anything backfires," Baker instructed. "Be careful. It's better to take your time—and be safe."

Green nodded and left.

* * * * * * *

The combination of the rum punch, the fiery heat of the sun, which baked down upon the small plantation patio, and the lovely woman sitting opposite him, filled Greg Hern with mixed emotions.

Carol Judson looked up at him; her inviting eyes making intimate suggestions that he wouldn't have ignored from a more mature woman.

"Enjoying your business vacation?" she inquired in a soft pleasant voice.

"I just arrived last night; give me time," he laughed, taking a deep puff from his cigar. He avoided focusing his attention on the woman by pressing out an imaginary wrinkle in his white silk trousers.

For the last twenty minutes they had been alone on the patio and Greg had watched the woman with growing interest, fascinated by her youthful innocence. At least this was his belief at the beginning—now he felt doubts. It was the first time he'd been alone with Carol Judson since his arrival. It was also the first time he'd seen her since she had flowered into attractive womanhood. She was wearing a white blouse, with neckline slightly dipped, showing white creamy flesh, which lent a subtle hint of seductiveness to her. The blouse pushed out in front, making no attempt to hide the jutting shape of her large breasts. The flaring gray skirt showed only the lower portion of her legs, enough to heighten his normal male interest. But it was Carol's expressive face that invited most of his attention. Her large eyes would twinkle one moment and suddenly veil over with smoldering desire. Then, abruptly, she would once again be the innocent young girl, daughter of his hosts.

"Want another drink?" Carol inquired, pointing a delicately tapered finger at the tall glass in front of him.

Greg nodded. "Not too strong. Heat and liquor are a powerful combination in the presence of such an attractive young girl."

Momentarily, anger spurted in Carol's eyes. "You still think of me as that little girl with a pony-tail!"

"Let's say that regardless of what I might like to believe, it would be impossible to deny you've matured into a very seductive woman," Greg quickly countered, smiling.

Carol reached for the large pitcher on the table at her side and filled his glass with the strong rum punch. Her eyes gazed deep into Greg's, twinkling with pleasure at his words. After a moment, she relaxed into the bamboo chair.

"What have you been doing with yourself in the past years, Carol?" Greg asked, hoping to direct the mood away from any kind of flirtatious exchanges.

"Been going to college. Last year." She shifted nervously, looking up at the bright disk of the sun.

"What're you going to do afterwards?" Greg sipped his drink, wishing it would sooth away the noon-day heat.

"I really don't know. Probably join the international set of young socialites. Live a little, and then maybe get married." Her eyes burned as they met his; there wasn't anything subtle about her gaze.

There were several moments of silence and then suddenly Carol said: "Gosh, it's hot!"

She unbuttoned the top of her blouse. The whiteness of her bra showed, catching Greg's eye.

10

They talked a little longer and then another button unlatched under her fingers.

Greg felt restless. The sight of those thrusting breasts brought his natural male interests to the edge of overpowering his resistance. It was difficult to avoid making a flirtatious comment. With another woman he would have done so. Even with Carol, if she wasn't the daughter of a close friend.

"Don't you think you should be a little more modest?" he inquired, trying hard to keep his eyes away from her breasts.

"Why? We're alone." Carol looked innocently into his eyes.

"Don't be coy."

"I'm not as innocent as you might think, Greg. And it's just as hard for a woman as for a man." Her eyes were stating much more.

Greg felt embarrassment. The idea of having an affair with Carol was far from unappealing.

He tried to change the subject. "What time shall we leave for the party tonight?"

"The Bedford? About seven."

Another button loosened itself. He could see the creamy, tanned flesh below her bra.

Their eyes suddenly met and for a long time the silence had a heaviness that was unsettling to his control.

Carol shrugged.

"It's damned hot!" she exploded.

Without warning her blouse slipped off creamy white shoulders.

Greg tensed before the lovely sight. Her skin was flawless ivory, darkly tanned ivory. Where the bra cupped her breasts he saw bulging flesh pushing

11

around it, as if overflowing the restraining cloth.

Damned women! He thought savagely, controlling the desire that began bubbling through him. *Why couldn't they act respectable? What'd they think he was?*

"We're alone," Carol announced in a breathy voice. There was no room for doubt as to what she wanted.

"Why don't you make a pass at me, Greg?" she breathed.

Her boldness unnerved him. Yet it shouldn't have been so unexpected. She was young, healthy, the daughter of a rich man, spoiled, demanding. For as long as he had known her, she went after what she wanted in a direct manner—and usually got it.

For a moment longer he was tempted and then nervously, reluctantly, he lowered his eyes.

"No, Carol," he forced his lips to say.

There was a stony silence. A long, hateful silence that seemed to reach out and squeeze its fingers around his neck.

He felt like a bastard. But he would have been even more of a bastard to have taken her offer. She was the daughter of his host; and for that reason, alone, he should avoid involvement with her on an intimate level.

When he looked up again, Carol wasn't there. She had left.

For a long time he sat there, angry with himself, and more angry with Carol. If she had been any other girl he wouldn't have hesitated a moment. He only hoped she never tried again, for anything that might happen between Carol and himself would be purely physical. There could be nothing romantic or beautiful about it. And no matter what the newspapers had printed about Greg's affairs, they had all been honest relationships with mature women—love affairs in every sense.

Shrugging, Greg sipped the drink and looked at the far horizon. His mind wandered to other thoughts, more important than involvement with women. Even the merger with Judson, which had brought him here, had little room in his thoughts. The merger could have been worked out by any flunky in his employ.

Momentarily his mental wanderings returned to Carol. He couldn't bring himself to think of her as anything other than an immature child; a young girl playing with her emotions—in love with love. This was the last kind of woman he wanted to become involved with.

It was a long time before he wandered back into the house, returning to the room the Judsons had given him for his stay on Temming.

* * * * * * *

The room was walled with bookcases. One section was on business and business law. There was a huge oak desk in the middle of the room and a large, comfortable dark brown leather chair in front of it.

John Judson, a large, rounded man, stepped behind the desk and sat in the cushioned chair. He pulled a couple of cigars from a small box and handed one to Greg.

"We don't have much time before going to the Bedford, but I learned something in town this afternoon," John said in a grim voice. There was a nervous air about the man as he leaned forward, puffing on his cigar. "Fats Delano is here, at the islands."

The statement dropped like a bomb.

Silence followed.

"I also heard that he's connected with Renton, Inc.—the very company we've been doing business with—and I'm frankly scared!" Judson nervously wiped his face, though it was bone dry. "He's connected with narcotics."

For a moment Greg hesitated and then said: "Look, John—there's nothing to worry about right now."

"I don't like it, Greg!" The words exploded and were final.

"I'm not the fool I might appear—"

"I never said anything like that, Greg. It's just that you aren't experienced in such matters. If your father were still living—he'd know how to handle things." Judson tapped the top of his oak desk with a finger and then fell back in his chair. "What are we going to do?"

"Well, to start with, John, I'm not going to do anything. I came here to arrange the merger with your State's firm so we could pull you out of the red—so...let me worry about Fats Delano!

"Look, the operations will be run under my company. We'll be handling the paper work—and the responsibilities. The exporting from the Orient will be taken care of by our head office. You'll be clear—so what's the problem?"

"What if Fats Delano's using Renton as a means to smuggle narcotics into the States? That puts us in a bad spot. It's bad enough we're doing business with them—who knows what they have pushed through already. Then if we sign—"

"Okay—if it'll make you feel better I'll have it looked into."

Judson sighed. "I was hoping you'd suggest that. I don't have all the money behind me that I used to. Do you have the money and the machinery to cover such a—?"

"Forget it," Greg told him, looking suddenly at his watch. It was 7:30. He was anxious to get to the party and meet Carl Bedford.

There was a long silence and then the den door opened and Mary Judson stood there.

"Are you men through with the important business?" the matronly woman asked, brushing back a lock of shock white hair from her wide, attractive forehead.

John's voice was light; but sounded forced. "Okay, honey—I guess we might as well leave."

"Where's Carol?" Greg inquired.

"She's not going. Has a headache," Mrs. Judson told him.

"I'm sorry." Greg knew that wasn't the truth. He was probably the only one in the house, other than Carol, who did.

Twenty minutes later they were at the Bedford home, several miles south of the Judson plantation.

OPERATION: DOUBLE-CROSS, BY CHARLES NUETZEL

CHAPTER TWO

The party was filled with the scent of island palms, roast pig staked over a huge pit of coals, and spiced rum punch served in coconut shells

Beyond this island theme, it was much like many such parties given all over the world. People stood around sipping drinks, talking about world problems, covering the war, speculating on survival in a war dominated by the threat of terrorism. Commenting on the latest Island gossip...

> Miss Landers is playing around with that native boy...did you hear about Ted—he's at it again...they say the fishing boats are having trouble making their way...I heard something about a storm coming up...The Bedfords give a good party, but I sometimes wonder about that woman!

On and on about subjects that nobody was really interested in. One exchange, a fiery argument, caught his attention for a few moments, for it touched on problems that might even affect Hern Industries.

"We can't just turn the other cheek in this world, today," a serious middle-aged man was saying. "The Islamic terrorists are fanatics, and we should bomb their home towns, make them pay a heavy price-tag."

"We can't do that," the slender woman next to him was saying. "That would be horrid. What about the children?"

"The children turn themselves into living bombs!"

"Oh, you're horrid!" she cried.

"Well, he's right," a third man countered. "We can't just stand there, doing nothing."

"We aren't. Iraqi is—"

"A mess," the woman pointed out. "But these are human beings."

Another, slightly slurred voice snapped: "I say...slit their throats and their...wives and every member of their...family...tribes, town..."

"They don't care about that. They believe they act in the name of Allah, and even their own wives and children are–"

"They're crazy," a voice spit out. "Trying to convert us—"

"Just like the Christian world is trying to convert the Muslims..."

"Screw all of them!"

At point Greg could resist saying: "Not all Muslims are terrorist! Very few are! In fact the rest of the Islamic world is filled with people trying to live their lives in peace. The Western world is using up their oil without any regard to their culture, and determined to convert them to our way of living, thinking and even religion. We're as damning and fanatic true believers as they are."

"Well, I don't care! There is no way to win a war of this kind, for either side, except the total destruction of civilization. They want to go back to the eighteenth, hell, maybe the sixteenth century."

At that point he lost interest and moved away.

It was all common enough to Greg Hern. The normal cocktail exchange that could take place anywhere in the world today. And a common problem the world faced, and world leaders could only try to contain it. Nothing could stop a lone fanatic from killing themselves or acting on their own. But at least grand, international movements could be crushed, in time, or at least held off while more sane people found realistic solutions.

He had talked to his host, but found nothing unusual about the man. Bedford was tall, gray haired, with a nervous twitch that worked his left cheek upwards when he talked; the nervousness rubbed off onto anybody watching him. But no vital information escaped his thin lips. He carried on polite social conversation. "How are you, Mr. Hern? I've heard a lot about you. Sure glad you could come to our party—I was hoping you'd be here." A few statements like that and Greg moved to the large table, which was spread with island foods, and more important, the large punch bowl with huge ice chunks floating in its reddish contents.

Greg was pouring himself another drink, thinking vaguely about Carol and feeling frustrated that it hadn't been possible to take her offer without awkwardly complicating things, when a tall redheaded female stepped up to him. It was her voice that drew his attention.

"You're Mr. Hern, aren't you?" she inquired in a low, husky voice.

For a moment he was captivated by her beauty. He just stood there looking at her in a daze.

She had a seductive quality about her half-hidden eyes that was far subtler than Carol and far more mature. Her figure was voluptuous, but neither childlike nor vulgar. It had just enough flavoring of raw sex appeal to lend her an air of mystery.

Finally he answered her.

"Yes, I'm Hern. I didn't realize I was so well known." Greg grinned, letting his eyes flow once more over her shapely body.

"You're quite well known. I've read about your escapades in the papers." Her voice was warm and low; intimate. There was a fullness to her lips that was both sensual and sensitive. With each word her mouth moved in a slightly crooked way; it was delightfully fascinating to watch.

"Quite a party the Bedford are putting on," Greg remarked, hoping to point the conversation away from himself and the reputation the papers had given him in the past three years since he'd inherited his father's vast industrial empire.

"Quite," she admitted, a smile moving her lips up at one corner. "My name is Linda. So now we're friends." This time her smile had sensual warmth. There was a shaded fiery interest in her eyes. "I hope you don't think me too bold having come up to you like this. Just that...well, I never expected to see you here at the islands. Business or pleasure?"

"A little of both," he threw back. "I'm staying at the Judsons'. Just arrived last night—they insisted I come to the party. I feel like a fish yanked out of the

20

sea."

Linda laughed, her eyes flashing with amusement. For a moment her white teeth showed. Then she was thoughtful, her lips compressed into a kissable pout. Her hand reached out impulsively, taking his. "Come along, we can get into the salt water you like so much."

He followed silently, pleased by the soft, yielding texture of her hand in his. They moved out across the patio and into the darkened garden beyond.

"There's a back entrance. We can slip out there. A short walk to the beach. I love the beach at night don't you?—especially when the moon's bright, like now. Don't you love the tropic nights? The perfumed scent, the flowers, the air?"

He nodded.

"You're quite a poet." He was about to say something else, but just then her hip softly brushed his and he wasn't quite sure how much control his voice would have. He remained silent.

They came to a brick wall, where a huge wooden gate was half open. Greg quickly swung it all the way back. As he followed the redhead down the narrow roadway toward the beach, Greg felt a throbbing excitement increase his pulse. There was something about this woman that immediately had attracted him; something more than just physical charm.

Maybe it was her eyes, he told himself.

The fresh smell of salt air was around them. The surf hitting the shoreline, sounded like angry thunder.

"Mind telling me something about yourself?"

Greg questioned, gently squeezing Linda's hand. She responded by gripping his fingers tightly between hers. It was silent and intimate, but even more than that. Something about the exchange seemed to communicate more than mere physical pleasure through him; and he was sure Linda felt it too.

When she was silent for a long while, he asked:

"You're the original mystery woman?"

Linda's head nodded quickly, whispering her long red hair against the silken green of her dress. "You hit it! The mystery woman." She seemed to like the idea. She paused and looked up into his eyes. "You don't mind, do you? After all, I came to you...and all that."

"Do I have a right to mind?" He put an arm around her waist and gently attempted to bring her body closer to his.

"No," Linda told him, pulling away and starting once more toward the beach.

They continued in silence until they came to the beach. It was then she turned to Greg and hurriedly said: "I hope you haven't gotten the wrong idea about me."

"About what?"

"Well—I don't want you getting the wrong idea about why I brought you out here—for a walk," Linda added lamely.

"Why did you suggest it? This is your show—from the beginning."

"I don't know. It just seemed to work out that way. I saw you there—and...well, I was standing in front of you talking and.... Maybe because I've always been a little too impulsive, as long as I can remember. Even as a child I used to get myself into

22

a lot of trouble because I was too impulsive. But... that's a different matter." She hesitated for a moment and then added: "Let's not talk!"

The ocean was breaking on the white sandy shore, each wave outlined with a string of sparkling diamonds as it moved up onto the sands. Then the emerald water slid reluctantly back into a new, freshly created string of shimmering jewels. The moon was a pale haunting disk in the night sky, surrounded by bright twinkling stars. There was a sultry warmth about the air that moved over him with caressing fingertips, building the romantic need, the physical desire to a demanding peak. Finally near the water's edge Linda sat down on the sand.

She looked up and smiled.

"Sit with me," she suggested in a small, breathless voice.

Greg sat down, trying to ignore her obvious charms, keeping his eyes off that lush body so nicely packaged to reveal much, but not too much. The nerves of his body were already edged by her nearness to a raw point.

"You staying on Temming long?" Linda inquired conversationally.

"That depends." He avoided a direct answer.

"On what?"

"A lot of things."

"You don't want to talk about it?" She looked into his eyes, searchingly. There was desire welling behind the controlled veil of her gaze.

"Not really." He patted her hand. "I'd rather talk about you."

"I'm just a young woman who has little to do. Nothing much of interest there." Linda suddenly

23

was avoiding his eyes.

They were silent for a moment. They listened to the waves move up the sand like arms reaching out for escape, only to be pulled back with a soft sigh.

"Will somebody be missing you?" Greg inquired.

He felt her hand tense in his at the question.

"I hope not," she answered softly.

"Then, there's a man?"

She lowered her gaze.

"No," she finally answered.

Linda was lying. He knew that.

"Maybe we should return," she offered a little nervously.

"Why? The night is young and the moon is high and the beach is a romantic place for two—"

Greg broke off because he'd almost said "Lovers," which at the last moment he realized didn't apply. But the hanging sentence didn't escape Linda's sharp mind.

"That's the trouble. It was foolish to come out here with you. We better return to the others before something happens that both of us might regret in the morning."

"I don't do anything I regret in the morning," he told her in a self-assured voice.

"I figured that out." Linda started to get to her feet.

For a second Greg didn't let go of her hand. He didn't want to lose the soft feel of it any sooner than necessary.

She paused until he released his fingers, then stood.

Looking up at Linda, highlighted in the glowing

24

moon, was a magnificent experience. Her breasts thrust out boldly against her dress. Her hair moved slightly in the evening breeze.

He was held captive to the view for some minutes and it was only her words that broke the magic and shattered the spell.

"Come on, let's get back."

Greg followed Linda up the beach, in the direction of the Bedfords' home. As he came to her, his hand reached out, quickly taking hold of her creamy white shoulder. The contact was surprisingly electric, sending little tantalizing pulses through every nerve.

She froze in reaction and half turned toward him. Their eyes met for a long time without moving. Something was happening that was very vital and electric.

They were both mature adults, fully aware of a mutual attraction that was amazingly strong. And the look in her eyes was raw, open desire, even if skillfully shaded, controlled. It wouldn't take much to spark it into an uncontrolled, raging fire. And at that moment he simply didn't give a damn about control. All he could think of was taking the obvious, silent offer, the quite plea. He knew she wanted him as powerfully as he wanted her.

Suddenly he jerked Linda into his arms. Her lips pressed lightly to his, and as her arms hesitantly slid around his neck, Greg felt her lips part and the deep probe of her delicate tongue surge hungrily out. It was like being connected to a live wire, jarring his body with a wildness impossible to contain.

The impact of the embrace left them both stunned, breathless. They clung to one another for some moments, breathing heavily. He could feel the throbbing beat of her heart as it pounded blood through her. Finally she gently moved away.

"That's what I meant," Linda murmured, huskily. She attempted to smile, but her lips wouldn't respond.

"We can't just drop it here!"

"Can't we?" Her arched eyebrows rose, creating a question of her features. "I don't know—I think it might be a good idea. To drop it. Before..."

Greg tried to reach for her again, but she slid away. "No—I'm going back—if you want to come with me...."

Greg nodded and they started for the Bedfords' huge plantation home. He didn't say anything until they reached the back gate that led to the huge garden.

"I'm sorry if I moved too fast back there," Greg apologized, his hand on her bare arm.

"Don't be. It was my fault. I started the whole thing. Just so we leave it there." She stepped through the gate, leaving him standing alone.

Greg pulled out a pack of cigarettes and lighted one. Later, after stepping on the butt, he moved slowly into the garden.

Linda had left loose raw ends that needed soothing. But there was no escape from the anguish. She was quite a charged woman.

Angrily Greg stepped across the garden to the low table and punch bowl. He poured a drink and turned his eyes to the surrounding people.

Forget women! he told himself. There are more important things to take care of. You shouldn't overdo the playboy routine.

26

* * * * * * *

Linda went up to her room right after leaving Greg Hern. She wanted to get drunk.

As she fixed herself a triple shot of raw whiskey from a bottle she kept in her nightstand, she felt an angry churning of guilt.

"Greg Hern is a damned nice guy. I didn't know it would be like this!" she whispered to herself. "It's a damned shame."

Linda hoped it didn't have to go any further. This game of international intrigue was new and bewildering to her. It wasn't the kind of thing she was used to.

Her past was filled with a lot of ugly experiences, nasty events that had been pretty much blurred during the last few years. She'd come up from the cheap side and worked her way into a plush deal, a neat, lovely life, which couldn't be threatened by anybody—not even a Greg Hern! As much as she was attracted to the man it might be necessary to play him all the way out, right into a dirty little snare. The hard fact was: she didn't have that much control over the situation. She wasn't the only one involved.

Damn! She thought, bitterly.

Her mood changed as she remembered that one fiery kiss. She ran her hands along her arms. Every nerve felt raw and aching.

God the man makes me hot all over! she realized, almost in pain at the thought of being with him again. If that happened it would be difficult to avoid wild, wanton intimacy. The desire was just that

27

fiery, raw and raging inside her.

She hadn't been kissed that way in months—too many months for her to remember.

CHAPTER THREE

The room was dim, the only light coming from the opened window. The two men were sitting in chairs, facing each other. The one doing most of the talking was huge, gross, hard. His lips snapped with every word like a reptile. His eyes were small and set deep in their sockets, staring out at the thinner man with a hint of distaste.

"I want this Hern brought into line." The fat man pointed a chubby tobacco stained finger at his listener. "You have to find out what he plans to do—and then see to it he does what *we* want. He knows I'm here and—he's heard about my connection with Renton."

With each word he pointed a stubby finger in the direction of the thin gray man sitting opposite him.

"We can't use force—not with a man like Hern! He doesn't scare easily!"

"Then find another way—I don't want to be bothered with the details! You've been given an assignment to do and I expect it to be done. And fast!" The fat man grinned. "I understand that Hern is quite a lady's man. Turn Linda on him again! Tell her to go as far as necessary—but find out exactly what he's doing here! I don't care what she has to do to get that information. Understand?"

The thin man looked nervously down at his hands. Sweat was forming on his narrow forehead. The haggard lines of his face seemed to tighten and slowly relax, only to tighten nervously again. His cheek twitched.

"Okay, then," he managed in a controlled voice.

"That's good, Bedford. You do it—and I'll do the rest!"

The two stood and shook hands.

Mr. Carl Bedford walked from the room. Ten minutes later he was in his small private sea plane with his wife, who had been waiting there for him.

"Get her up, George!" he told the pilot. Then leaning tiredly back, he turned his attention to the woman.

"The worse!" he announced in a dead, high voice.

"What a rotten world!" her voice cursed, bitterly.

"I don't like it either. But what can we do? You don't play around with the Big Man. You can't imagine what he is able to do to people. I've heard the rumors, and I've seen some of the...horrors. We don't need that kind of problem. Anything is better than that. There isn't a damned thing I can do about it. He had me hanging over a snake pit."

"I liked Greg," she said softly.

"So you liked him! You don't think I want to throw you into his arms, do you? You got into the marriage with your eyes wide. You were a little tramp in a cheap island saloon. You weren't an innocent baby. I pulled you out and put you into the

30

rich world you wanted to belong to. I needed a wife for social face—but one that I could trust! You wanted a large bank account and social position. Now the time's come for the payoff. And for me to pay Mr. Fats Delano for the extra business he's given me." There was harsh hatred in the man's words, mixed with bitter defeat. "It has become a dirty, scary, dangerous business...and it's gotten out of hand. But there's nothing I can do about it other than...try to survive!

"As for you—us—well...this marriage has always been a business arrangement. Not that I don't care...about you...in fact the only thing I care about is you and—"

"Please, Carl. You know how I feel about that!" she told him in an icy voice. "Like you said: you needed a wife—so we made a business arrangement. Leave it at that!"

They were silent for a long time, and as the plane circled over Temming Island, Carl Bedford said: "Look—think of it this way: Greg Hern has been using women for years as if they were products on sale at the nearest supermarket. He's the spoiled son of a rich man—and has played it that way. You've had to deal with men like that for years...before I knew you. Well, actually, nothing like him. But you know what I mean. Men want women like you. And you learned how to used that lovely body of yours to get where you are today. Now it's pay-off time. He has no ethics and is coldly savage in business deals. And not at all, according to his reputation with women, against taking any lovely toy to bed and making use of her body for a momentary pleasure. Don't be taken in by his charm. If he knew what you were up to—he'd smash your pretty brains!"

"I don't think he's that kind of man. I believe he's well—*to hell with it!*"

The plane circled down toward the blue ocean below and then started to skim close to the water. Finally a splash of foam waved behind them as the plane broke the surface.

"Linda, look—just try to pump him for information, first. If there's any indication of...that he's going to pull out of the deal with Renton—then we'll know what to do."

"Okay! *Okay!*" she shouted angrily, hating herself. "Whatever you say. Anything you say. I'll send a note to him in the morning! But just shut up!"

The plane rushed in toward the shore, taxied to the dock and then finally settled to a stop.

* * * * * * *

At the Judson's, breakfast was served on the patio. Carol had been first up, and her father was sitting waiting to be served when Greg joined them. They were in the middle of devouring a delicious meal of ham and eggs, home-fried potatoes, orange juice, and coffee. The maid came to Greg and handed him a small letter. He looked calmly at the little pink envelope with its neat, tiny feminine handwriting on it. Nobody at the table said anything about it at first. There was little question in his mind as to who had sent it.

There was a long, heavy silence, a stilted silence, as if each person sitting at the table were aware of what the note said.

32

"Never can tell when you might get private mail," Greg managed, weakly, finding it hard to raise his eyes from the table.

Carol's laugh was nervous. "Looks like our man Hern's been making points with some lady." Then she added a little harsh, cutting word: "*Already!*"

Mr. Judson looked up, his eyes darting to Carol. He was silently questioning.

Carol looked down at her plate.

The rest of the meal was a study in awkward silence, lacking mention of the note, lacking any of the bright levity which had been present before it came. Greg was glad when it was over.

That's the trouble with society: too nosey! Greg thought, when the meal was over and he had finally managed to gain the privacy of his room.

He tore at the envelope. It read:

> Greg, I can't let things stay the way they are. I'm impulsive, as I told you. Impulse started this thing.
>
> Careful thought has finally managed to do nothing to talk me out of seeing you again. I *must* see you!
>
> I'll be at Ben's Inn at 2:00 this afternoon. If you are still interested, meet me there.
>
> Linda

He looked at the careful, feminine handwriting, considering if he should continue a relationship with a woman he hardly knew. It was good cover, but it could get involved and messy. The balancing act between his business dealings and the playboy reputation that had to be maintained was delicate. And, he had to admit that Linda was one hell of a woman!

His mind conjured up the image of her lovely face, her mature, interesting eyes—he relived those moments with her on the beach, feeling the emotions that had surged through him.

Greg knew he had to see her, too.

Just then there was a knock on his door. For a moment he hesitated and then said: "Yes?"

"It's Carol. Can I come in? I want to talk to you."

Sighing, Greg opened the door. Carol stood there, charmingly smiling at him. Then the young woman walked in, and very firmly closed the door behind her. The light scent of perfume clouded around her. It was delicate and sensual.

Carol looked up into his eyes. Her lips were half parted, as if awaiting a kiss; as if every nerve and energy in her body were focused on the need to be swept up into his arms. Then she slowly shook her head and stepped away.

"I wanted to explain about the other afternoon."

Her voice was brisk, impersonal now. "I want you to understand why—"

"There's nothing to explain," Greg offered, almost embarrassed.

"Yes there is!" Carol stated firmly. Her lips compressed in momentary thought and then finally she continued. "I'm not the kind of person who throws herself at a man, like I did the other day—it was just that I wanted to—"

"It was hot—and there were the drinks. Just say the mood seemed right. And—well...." He shrugged

34

his broad shoulders helplessly.

What could he really tell her? That she had made a fool of herself? No! Or that he'd love nothing more than to toss her onto the bed and ravish that lovely young body? Hardly!

"Don't think I wasn't serious," she quickly assured him. "I was just a damned fool—the way I went about it. That's what I wanted you to know."

Silence was awkward. Greg felt sorry for her, because she was once again making a fool of herself. She was all talk—didn't know how to handle the situation. "Look, Carol. You're attractive, even beautiful. Any man would willingly marry you—or take what you're trying to offer. But—well, to be honest, this isn't the place or the time."

For a moment anger flamed in her eyes. She stood in front of him, her breasts heaving, her lips parted as if to say something. It took seconds for the words to form. "What do you think I am? A baby? For God's sake—you don't leave much room for pride in a woman, do you? What do you want me to say—how can I convince you—admit there've been men in my life? Is that what you need to hear? Or that I like a good healthy...you know what? Is that what you have to hear? Damn it all, Greg! I know what kind of man you are. What do you think? It's hard for a woman, too. A woman has...desires. And I've...grown up since we saw each other last!" She broke off, aware that her words had gone too far, that she had once more stumbled into desperate pleading—pleading to a man who had already turned her down. Tears welled in her eyes and her lips trembled.

"Carol—please. Try to understand...."

"Damn you! What's wrong with me? What have you against me—beside my parents?" she blurted. She stood there, her fists doubled at her side, her eyes pleading with his.

How easy it would be to take advantage of her. They were in his room, the door closed. Nobody would enter without being invited. They were as safe as in some distant hotel room. How easy to simply sweep her off her feet and totally possess the gift she was begging him to take.

"There's nothing wrong with you, Carol," he told her gently as he could. "Like I said, you're more than attractive—and more of a temptation than I like to admit. But let's try to keep things under control. This isn't a new toy you're playing with. This isn't a game you're experienced enough to handle!"

Carol wiped teams from her cheek. "I'm tired of control. I've had a crush on you since we first met. And believe me I don't plan to let it lie there—" She broke off, her eyes looking at the note still clutched in Greg's hand. "Don't underestimate me, Greg. I usually get what I go after! And, quite frankly, I've been...quite excited about you coming here. I figured it was about time you got a chance to know me as a woman...you only know the little girl I used to me. Don't make the mistake of thinking you can brush me off like...like a little girl. I'm all woman, and I want you to know it!"

"I don't underestimate you."

Her eyes were lingering on the note.

"I think you had better leave, before John or Mary find out you're in my bedroom. It might not look so good," Greg suggested, staring meaning-

36

fully at the door. "We wouldn't want them to get the wrong impression."

For a moment Greg thought Carol was going to lose control again. She was on the verge of tears; tears of frustration. Then her features froze over. Her eyes filled with cold determination, and another emotion that almost bordered on hate.

"Now, come on, Carol, be a nice…lady!"

"Well, put that way…" She suddenly recovered, laughed at that. "Daddy would be surprised…but mum? Well she's not stupid. She knows how men look at me. And she knows I'm been around the…well, barn a few times. So there!"

Then after a long moment she jerked around and stomped out of the room, slamming the door after her.

Greg sighed his relief and changed for his meeting with Linda.

* * * * * * *

Ben's Inn was a small saloon with the stale smell of sweaty bodies and cigarette smoke. It wasn't the kind of place that Greg might have expected Linda to pick. Yet as he looked at the dimly lit room with its dark, oak bar counter that spanned the full length of the long narrow saloon, he realized the cheapness was probably the reason for Linda having suggested the place. Nobody either of them socialized with would come here.

This was a place for native help, for the lower class workers and fishermen who worked and lived on the island.

It took Greg several minutes to accustom his

eyes to the dark surroundings. For a moment he couldn't find Linda, then he spotted her red hair. She was sitting in a lone booth, smoking nervously. Her eyes spotted him and for a moment a smile formed on her lips.

As Greg stepped forward, he felt the curious eyes of several men, who were sitting at the bar, follow his progress down the length of the room. They stared at his finely pressed, expensive white linen suit. He quickly slipped into the booth opposite Linda.

"Hoped you'd make it," was her simple greeting.

Instantly a lovely wave of total joy rushed into him, as their eyes met. It was as if two long time lovers were meeting after a long wait, a lingeringly period of overwhelming mutual desire. It hardly made sense; for they were really total strangers. Yet this kind of thing had happened with a special women—an instant desire that reached deeply into his very being, so completely it was as if they were both part of the same soul, finding one another. It wasn't serious love so much as serious passion mixed with real caring. A connection as deeply powerful as it was possible to have with a total stranger. Some called it love at first sight; though it was more mutual animal desire at first glance—and instant liking and instant connection that took in their total beings in one hungry gulping embrace.

There was a short silence as he took a cigarette and lit it. His eyes moved over Linda's figure. She was dressed in an old, loose fitting blouse and flaring blue skirt, much as the fishermen's wives and daughters might have worn. She appeared to fit into this place as naturally as any of the fishermen and dock workers. Her hair was flowing freely over her shoulders, not quite neatly combed. To all outer appearances she seemed to be one of the lower class inhabitants of the island.

He was already fired by simple raw desire for this woman. And she was making no effort to keep from being seductive. In fact, one instant glance into her eyes left no doubt. Verbal conversation was almost meaningless, for the visual subtext was so powerfully tangled in their obvious longing for one another. Yet the word-play had to be acted out, so they could move to the next stage.

"Received your note at breakfast," he lamely stated, in an awkward attempt to begin a conversation, to cut through the stilted quiet. She took a deep nervous drag from her cigarette and gazed steadily into him. Her eyes, as they met his, were smoldering with raw desire—yet with something else, too. Finally, Linda asked, "Want a drink? I don't think it'd be good to stay here without having something."

She indicated her beer sitting on the table before her.

"We have to stay?"

"For a while. You attracted enough attention in that suit. It would be bad to leave right away. I don't want everybody on the island to know what's going on—it'll be hard enough to keep things quiet." There was a heavy defeat in her voice, as if she had been fighting an inner battle, and lost.

Greg ordered beer. They waited in silence until the drink came. Once the barman had left, Greg lifted the glass to his lips and sipped. There was a salty dryness to the beer, and it had a flat stale taste.

"What now?" he inquired. It wasn't his nature to let a woman take the lead, but he reluctantly realized it was her play—and "playground." He didn't know the rules; she did.

Linda was thoughtful for a moment, then said: "Even on an island like this it is possible to make certain arrangements."

Greg nodded. "Where?"

"There's a place I know."

They waited in silence for a few minutes and then Greg stood, staying, "Let's get out of here!"

Linda hesitated before standing.

They walked through the narrow streets of the tiny settlement. The small shops with their low roofs and grim window displays seemed grotesquely depressing. The people, dark skinned, either by the tropic sun or by native coloring, half naked, gave the atmosphere a weird color that seemed negative for a romantic mood.

Everything seemed awkward, out or sorts.

There was only the raw sexual energy that even now seemed to flow warmly between them like the exchange of a tropic breeze.

Neither of them said anything until they had walked several blocks. And when the conversation opened up a little, it, too, was somewhat awkward, as if floundering in its attempt to find a solid anchor to let things develop naturally into a romantic interlude. Then Linda turned to Greg, looking nervously into his eyes.

"That wasn't such a good meeting place, after all, was it?" She smiled, flirtatiously. "Hardly a good start for a romantic interlude between strangers."

40

"No—not really," he admitted. "Hardly that."

"I couldn't think of any other place..." Her voice paused and her wide eyes stared up into his. "This all seems sorta awkward now. I don't mean—well, maybe you know what I mean." She sounded desperate, and he felt sorry for her.

"Forget it. We're together. That's all that counts." He put his arm around her shoulder. "Strangers or not. I certainly want to get to know you better."

"Now you're sounding quite seductive," she murmured with some humor. "I'm shocked!"

"I somehow doubt that."

"Ah, but I'd imagine you're shock-proof."

"What makes you say that?"

"You have a reputation, you know."

"Reputations can be distorted."

"Well...I hope yours isn't quite as distorted as you so modestly suggest," she laughed, letting her hip brush his. "I hardly think you're...well, inexperienced with women."

"I never suggested that."

"What're we talking about?" she suddenly said, almost serious. Then smiling offered: "Come on— my car is down the street."

"Are you making a pass at me? I'm horrified!" he chuckled.

"I thought that was the man's part."

"Hardly. Any man with any experience knows it is the woman who does the seducing."

"Now where didn't you get such a foolish idea?"

"Like you said, I have a reputation to uphold."

"And I know where to find out just how much

that rep holds up to reality. The place is not too far from here. A private lodge. Owned by Mr. Bedford. I'm—a friend of his. He has a key hidden under the front mat. We could go there—nobody uses it very often. Only when he has guests."

"Why not your place?" Greg inquired.

"Don't be silly! We can't. I'd rather not talk about it!"

"You sure we can use Mr. Bedford's place?"

"Completely," she announced, gripping his hand and urging him to follow her.

* * * * * * *

The lodge was built along the island style of one floor covered by a palm roof. That was merely the outer, visual trimming; the design, the dressing, for the construction was firm and solid. It was modernly furnished and had a huge stone fireplace in the large living room. There were a couple of bedrooms in the back of the lodge.

Greg built a fire and Linda mixed a couple of drinks, then they settled on the large studio couch. By then the earlier awkwardness had mellowed and they seemed suddenly quite relaxed, like two old friends. She nestled against him, his arm around her, his hand caressing the soft texture of her shoulder.

"I still feel wrong about this. Taking another man's place—drinking his liquor," Greg said uneasily. It was only half a lie.

"Believe me—there's nothing to worry about. We can easily replace the liquor—and he'd be pleased to learn I'd used the lodge. Take my word for it—there's nothing to worry about!" After a pause, Linda giggled. "Anyway you have enough money to buy and sell Bedford over and over again—without feeling it."

Greg nodded. "Okay—I won't talk about it anymore. Just being socially polite, anyway."

As he looked at the woman sitting next to him, it wasn't hard to recapture the feeling of romantic interest, the physical desire that had moved him the first night. A very natural animal appeal seemed to flow generously between them, embracing, enveloping their two bodies within a soft, warm embrace. Some people could connect like that. He felt very close to Linda in a very special way. Animal, sensual, sexual. And something else, less easy to define.

They sat for a long time, sipping their drinks. The relaxing mood shifted, subtly became more intimately warm. Greg's hand caressed hers, gently, tenderly, as he gazed into her soft eyes.

"Everything's happening so fast—I guess we both feel it," Greg whispered.

"Yes—but that happens." Linda hesitated and then suggested: "Maybe we shouldn't have come."

The statement hung there between them, incomplete.

Greg placed a tender finger on her full lips. The softness of her mouth fired the sensual desire to kiss her. But it wasn't the right moment.

Linda pressed herself gently to him, clinging like a little child, as if taking in the nearness with all that was within her. Verbal conversation wasn't necessary. Just their nearness said it all; the touches, contact. They were like two people who had loved for an eternity, and knew the pleasure of one an-

43

other's total being and were at the moment content to simply engage in the quiet of one another, the nearness, the very reality of simply being. Each of them knew what would follow, but were almost hungrily clinging to the immediate mood, the sense of knowing one another. For it was this time together, silently listening to one another's very existence, one another's breath itself, that was a total fulfillment. They were awaiting the moment when their mutual oneness had reached a peak beyond which there was no control. Yet neither seemed in a hurry to rush things. They simply wanted to be together, aware, letting it all happen at its own lovely speed. Each breath seemed a union all its own. It was, in a way, a secret, lovely ecstasy, compete in itself.

Several times they look into each other's eyes and that became an exquisite union, as if some mystical magic were joining them in more than a physical way, as if their very souls were intermingling, meshing, caressing, and linking.

At one point he murmured: "You're so lovely."

Later she brushed her head against he check, her hair flowing softly. "I wish it could be like this forever."

Her words were soft, musical, and seemed to caress into him so tenderly, gently. None of it made sense, but yet it made all the sense in the world. And the foreplay was simply this prolong togetherness. They were communicating on a level far beyond anything banal, obtaining a level of oneness that reached far above the physical and into something far richer, far more meaningful and a complete in itself. They were lovers about to discover the full meaning of their mutual need and desire and feeling for one another.

It was dark outside before the mood changed, before the nearness of the woman finally demanded that first kiss that was to race their mutual need into a demanding sexual hunger.

The liquor had now created an odd dream-like feeling, and he abruptly found himself hungrily taking in the lovely shape of her. The large thrust of her breasts, the white cream of her throat, the voluptuous curves of her body. Then without really knowing he'd done so, she was gripped in his arms, their lips were trembling against one another.

The first embrace was hot, rapid fire, burning through them, whipping their desires raw. Her tongue, moist and warm as wine, surged deep into his mouth with such hunger that left his head swimming in the pleasure of her. The kiss was like liquid nectar, like a tonic of passion that raised their desires to volcanic pressures.

Then came the endless mutual caressing that left them naked, flushed with so much need, hunger, that they greedily embraced, clinging together, unmoving at first, then slowly, deliciously, discovering one another, exploring, sharing anxious kisses. Then gently, step by step, they were lifted higher and higher into a fury of passion. Then it became a ravishing madness, yet utterly gentle in its mutual giving. In the final moments they were locked together in a wildly tender moment of ecstasy and were bathed in wave after wave of warm release. And it was a form of love, a wonderfully sense of mutual need that washed through them with overwhelming power. Only then did they drift into a semiconsciousness in one another's arms.

A long time later Greg fixed drinks and sat down beside Linda.

The woman was silent for a while and then asked in a low, fear-controlled voice: "How long do we have? How long will you be here at Temming? How long is our moment together?"

Greg felt a tightening constrict his throat. He couldn't look into her eyes. Suddenly he didn't want it to end—a strange realization. But he simply knew this couldn't be a one-night stand. He wanted to be with her again.

"Let's not think about that," he said softly.

CHAPTER FOUR

It was well past three in the morning when Linda dropped Greg where he'd parked his car. The town was silent in its dark blanket of sleep. It was like being in a dead world. The sky was black and overcast, the stars were dimmed out. The moonlight was a mere glow behind ink-black clouds. He started the engine and slowly drove out of town.

His mind was reliving the hours with Linda, wondering exactly what was happening between them. He'd never really had any woman hit him like that before.

If his mind hadn't been preoccupied with such thoughts it would have been more alert to what happened next, and he might not have reacted the way he did.

Somewhere between town and the Judson plantation, at a bend in the road, a man stood, waiting with a flare in his hand. When Greg's car came into sight the man moved into the middle of the road.

Greg saw the waving light and slammed on his brakes.

He leaned out the window "What's the trouble?"

A harsh voice sounded from the foliage at his left. "Get out of the car!"

It was a moment before Greg's mind recognized the threat in the voice. Impulse suggested speeding away, but logic told him that a bullet would travel faster than a car.

"Get out—fast!"

Slowly he opened the door and stepped onto the road. His gut tightened and every muscle tensed, ready.

"Come here—into the brush!" came the second command. Greg stepped forward. The man who had been waving the flare was stepping in behind him. He heard a sigh of relief. Then: "He's the one!"

Before Greg could do anything, something slammed at the back of his head and he staggered forward, stunned, stars flashing in front of his eyes. He tried to gain control, tried to raise his arms to defend himself. But another object smashed his face, and he buckled backwards into waiting arms that clamped his tightly behind him.

Greg couldn't see the men, only shadowy images in the darkness before him. He was trying to clear his vision when a fist sank deep into his gut. Another blow on the back of his neck sent him to the ground.

"That'll teach you!" a voice snarled as a boot pushed Greg's face deep into the soft ground. "Teach you good!"

Greg struggled to keep conscious, fought to gain his feet. He trembled on shaky arms, straining. But the muscles wouldn't work fast enough.

Something kicked into his ribs.

Greg jerked off balance, falling over on his back. Another booted foot connected with his head and this time a terrible sick blackness closed in on

48

him, spinning around and around dizzily, then slowly drifted over the last dim consciousness.

Suddenly he was aware of blaring light blinding his eyes. Greg heard a moan and realized it came from his own throat. He tried to move and for several moments he couldn't. Then muscle by muscle he tensed, forced himself into a sitting position, and then opened his eyes.

For a moment he couldn't understand what had happened. Why was he sitting in the middle of a road, the sun blazing down on him like a choking blanket? He couldn't remember what happened last. *He'd been with Linda and then...she'd left him off at town. He'd been driving and...stopped...been beaten up....*

Memory ebbed back like the movement of molasses. With every thought came awareness of pain, throbbing pain that grated every nerve like raw fire. It was some time before he moved. His hands went carefully over his body, touching sensitive ribs, feeling, probing to see if anything had been broken. Once he assured himself that everything was fairly well in place, he stood. He was sore as hell, but no serious damage had been done. The mugging had been skillful.

Greg examined his surroundings, looking for the car. It only took a quick sweep of his eyes to discover it was missing.

Some damned kids out for kicks and wanting to see what they could get away with! Was his first thought. Then he reconsidered. No. It went deeper than that.

For one thing, this wasn't the States where a person could disappear with a car. On Temming an island a little less than ten miles across and twenty miles long, it would be impossible to disappear with something as large as a car. The police wouldn't find it too hard to discover the location of the car and who had taken it. Given time they would easily locate vandals.

So, he realized, *that was out.*

Then he remembered something the voice had said: "That'll teach you!"

Then what had really taken place? he wondered.

The only thing he could think of was something involving Linda. Unless Fats Delano had been responsible. But that was utterly fantastic. The man had no reason; at least none he could actually know about.

Linda was the only logical choice. A lover, boy-friend, or maybe a husband? That last thought numbed Greg clear into the depths of his bones. But that was fantastic, too.

Greg shook his head and started down the road toward the Judson plantation. It was a little over a twenty-minute walk, with every step a study in agonized pain. His mouth was dry, thirsty, his mind was crying for a drink to numb the soreness. With every step, fury burned through him; fury at whoever was responsible for his mugging. When he arrived at the Judson home, he was seething.

Carol was the first to greet him. She had been walking through the hallway when he stepped into the large bungalow. At the sight of him she expressed shock on her face, rushing forward.

"What happened?" she cried. "God, what happened?"

Greg waved aside the question with an irritated

jerk of his hand, asking: "Could you get me a drink?"

"Scotch?" she asked in a small voice, her eyes lowering to the floor.

"Who gives a damn? Anything you can find." He started for his room. "Be back in a little while."

A shower to clean away the dirt and sooth his muscles had settled his anger, and by the time he stepped into the drawing room, John and his wife had joined their daughter. They stood when he came in, but said nothing. Greg took the glass of Scotch from Carol's hand and then he sat down in a large leather chair.

There was a long stilted silence before anybody spoke and Greg managed to finish most of his drink by then.

"What happened?" John inquired, his voice concerned.

"I don't know, exactly. Somebody stopped me on the road, I was ordered out of the car and then given a first-class beating." Greg downed the rest of his Scotch and stood, stepped over to the small bar, poured himself another shot and then turned his eyes to the others. "The car's gone. I'll make good for that."

Judson shrugged. "Doesn't matter. But who did it?"

Greg slowly shook his head. "I wish I knew. They seemed to know me—or at least somebody said, 'That'll teach you'—or something like that."

Mary Judson looked at the bruises and then worried her face into a frown. "Can I call a doctor?"

"No—I'm all right." Silence met his statement. John broke it with: "You think it's connected with—"

Greg frowned him to silence. "I don't know what it's connected with—the car's gone. That's *all* I know!"

Carol's pretty face frowned, her eyes filled with irritation.

"What were you doing yesterday?" she demanded.

"Business."

She glared at him and then stood, fists tight on her hips. She looked like a wonderful child who had matured too young. Her face was so child-like that Greg wanted to step over to her and place a comforting arm around her. The womanly shape of her body, clothed in a tight gray skirt and loose, open blouse, made it impossible to really believe that fantasy. She was a woman in heat, determined to have him—and the jealousy flaring in her eyes revealed the emotions that were storming in her brain. She stood there for a moment and then stomped out of the room.

John coughed nervously and then said: "It's none of my business—but maybe you should take the warning."

Greg shot his eyes toward the older man. He wasn't in the mood for a lecture.

Judson shifted in his seat, said: "Well, things do get around on this island pretty fast."

Mary took a deep breath and hurried out of the room, embarrassment flushing her face.

"What're you getting at?" Greg demanded, feeling ice form along his spine. He quickly finished the Scotch and poured another.

"Greg—everybody knows your reputation with

52

the ladies," Judson pointed out in a high, nervous voice.

"It's over-rated." Greg began to feel the effects of the drink for the first time.

"Well believe me—I shouldn't butt in. But I think I know why someone might have hired those two men. It's not a good idea to play around with another man's wife, Greg."

For a startled moment he didn't know what to say. Then blurted: "What're you talking about?"

"You and Linda Bedford."

"You're crazy!" Greg exclaimed. But he realized his voice was too shaken to hold any conviction.

No wonder she could use the Bedfords' lodge, his mind screamed. His mouth felt dry and tasted sour with bitterness. He gulped the rest of the drink.

Anger ripped through him and then ebbed away. Carl Bedford had been within his rights. He might have gotten away with murder under the circumstances. Greg was just lucky he wasn't dead.

Lifting his eyes up to Judson he sighed tiredly. Then without another word he left the drawing room and walked out onto the back patio. His mind swam with confusion, sick defeat. The first woman that he'd ever found overwhelmingly important to him, a woman who with only two meetings had taken complete control over his emotions and mind, was married. All throughout his affairs he'd made it a hard practice to never play around with married women—now, at last, things had caught up around him.

Goddamned women! he cursed inwardly. *They were all bitches in heat!*

The anguish of discovering Linda's identity blinded him to the fact that Carol was sitting at the patio table, smoking a cigarette.

Her voice cut into his thoughts.

"Was it worth it?" she inquired acidly.

"What?"

Carol hesitated and then sighed. "Never mind. I guess I don't have the right to complain. I don't have a claim on you. So get yourself busted up a bit!" She laughed a little shrilly. "It serves you right!"

Greg wanted to be alone, but saw no reason to hurt Carol any more than necessary. "It wasn't what you think."

"How do you know what I think?" she demanded, staring icily at him.

"Let's drop the subject." He turned away from her, angry. It wasn't any of her business to pry into his private affairs; it wasn't anybody's damned business.

He heard Carol stand and then she came up behind him. Before he could do anything to stop her, he felt her arms slide around his waist and her body press to his back.

"Why don't you like me?" she murmured. "I'd be good for you—honestly—believe me. I'd be good. You'd like me. And I'm not married—I'm not tied up. I'm free—all you have to do is take me—please, Greg, I want you so much."

Greg felt sick nausea. It was a mixture of feelings, both of physical desire for Carol and the disappointment in the way she shamelessly threw herself at him. Like a cheap little slut in heat; or a child pretending to be a vamp!

He turned, disengaging himself from her. "Carol—you know how I feel about you."

"What's wrong with me?" she demanded shakily.

"Nothing. Nothing at all."

"Then why? I'm old enough to know my own mind. And it wants you, Greg. It wants you!"

"Let's not talk about it. You're too young and innocent." Greg realized that last remark had been a mistake. No woman wanted to know a man thought her too young or innocent when she wanted something that was completely opposite from innocent. But it was too late to retract.

Carol's face flared red and for a moment she stepped closer, glaring at him. "What do you know? You haven't even kissed me!"

Without warning she moved against him, her hips thrusting forcefully to his. Before he could stop her, she crushed her lips to his mouth, open and wide, her tongue reaching deep past his lips.

He couldn't help responding. It was impossible to ignore such an approach. Without wanting to he found his arms sliding automatically around her young body, crushing it closer, exciting to its full supple feel.

The kiss was electric.

Where Linda inspired tenderness, Carol created a savage demand on him. She literally "raped" him of all resistance. She wiggled against him and giggled.

Finally they broke away.

"You're hot!" she stated. "Really so…big!"

He stared at Carol, amazement blanching his face. Every indication in past days had told him she

55

wasn't necessarily innocent, yet this was completely unexpected. That kiss stripped naked the reality of her desire and those words left nothing for the imagination. There wasn't any doubt now about her not being a virgin. No woman who has never had a man before knew how to kiss that way.

You're a damned fool, he told himself, *and you should have taken her that first afternoon.*

"What do you think about my 'innocence' now?" Carol challenged. "How does that..." she lowered her gaze meaningfully, "little guy down there...well, it isn't so little any more, is it?"

She giggled in delight. "I want you even more."

"Maybe I misjudged you," he admitted honestly, the shock still numbing his mind. His lips wanted the softness of hers next to them again, his body wanted to feel the supple fullness of her pressing against it. Every nerve cried for her.

They stared at one another for a long time and then she finally said in a low, throaty voice, "I guess I'm different from other women—sometimes I need a man....terribly. And you make me feel so...hot all over. I need you, Greg. I need you desperately. I don't care how I get you! I don't care about pride or anything. Please, won't you stop this childishness? I'm a woman and I'm needy, and I'm fired to the limits...by what I felt against me! Do you want me to say it any more bluntly? I can, you know!"

Just then John Judson stepped out onto the patio.

"Greg, could you come with me. Something's come up. Something important." The man's face was white and drawn.

Greg turned and after a nod to Carol followed her father off the patio. He was glad for the interruption for now he realized it might have been a mistake to submit to her obvious desires. A raw, sexual, animal desire ripped at his guts. There had been, something in Carol's eyes, something in her expression that hinted at more than mere physical need for him. She had admitted to having had a crush on him for a long time. A teenage crush was one thing; a woman's passion quite another.

As much as he hated to admit it, he was afraid of Carol—afraid of getting involved too deeply. She was a spoiled and overly romantic girl, seeking thrills, but also hunting for the perfection of love. If she mixed it all up in her head, that could be a mess he didn't need to tangle with. There were too many willing women around to satisfy any of his more basic male needs. He didn't want complications. And he was already involved in one he hadn't realized was so complicated: Linda. He couldn't help believing that Carol wouldn't find it easy to stop after a one night stand, and that was the only way he could think of her. A one night stand to soothe the normal male need for a very beautiful and desirable woman who was throwing herself at him. She had already seduced him into wanting her, into accepting the possibility that they would, given the right chance, end up screwing each other's brains out.

John Judson led him into the den and closed the door behind them.

OPERATION: DOUBLE-CROSS, BY CHARLES NUETZEL

CHAPTER FIVE

Linda was sitting in the living room with her husband. They had just finished breakfast and Carl Bedford had lighted his pipe and was settling down to the mood where he would be questioning her about the night before. His right cheek nervously twitched and it was some time before he turned his tired eyes toward her.

"Well, what happened?" he questioned taking a puff from the pipe.

"I told you that I couldn't get any information. I told you last night. What else do you want?" she demanded defensively.

Every nerve in her body was raw from the sleepless night which had followed after having left Greg Hern. The experience had been far more unsettling than she could have ever imagined. Something very wild and wonderful had taken place and she was totally off-balance, unable to come to terms with her feelings. The man was wonderful, a fantastic lover. What she had believed would be nothing more than a wham bam interlude, all raw sexual energy between to adult beasts in heat, had turned into something so stunning different that it was literally shattering. They had shared a special moment, a slice of time so full and real and alive and rich with so many undercurrents that it left her breathless. It was like a fantastic romantic interlude, like something out of an amazing movie—filled with too much power, too much energy, too much of everything to be simply swept away as illusion. What they had shared was real. But real what? Certainly passion. Lust. All the biological stuff slammed into such an explosion of mutual pleasure that she could still feel him inside her. She would never forget that feeling he had inspired. It would haunt her for as long as she lived.

She studied her husband, a rich man who was merely a business arrangement. That was the cold-blooded fact of life. And she accepted this reality, even though it simply didn't fit into what she'd experienced with Greg.

"I'm sorry," she stated, then quickly added, in order to redefine the meaning of those two words: "I just don't have anything else to tell you."

"Why?" he pushed, slowly leaning forward and peering into her eyes.

"I just couldn't get any information. I couldn't get any thing from him. You'll have to take my word for it."

"Okay! Okay!" he growled, pulling the pipe from his face. "So, you couldn't get any information. What happened? Why couldn't you? Delano won't be interested in just taking my word for it. He'll need reasons why it takes so much time. He's not a patient man—and time's all important might now."

"Carl—it wasn't my fault. I couldn't come right out and ask, 'What're your plans about the exporting deal?' Or: 'Let me know your business secrets.'

He's not about to tell anybody his private affairs. All I can do is play it slowly—maybe a little hint will drop. He won't even let me know how long he's planning to stay. He's like a clam!" Linda bit at her lower lip and then dropped her eyes.

It wasn't possible to tell this man the truth. Under other circumstances it might be possible to believe that she had fallen in love with this strange wonderful man named Greg Hern. Linda was too experienced and hardened by life to believe that fairy tale. The harsh reality was that two people had met, had a fantastic night of it and that was the beginning and end. Nothing could come of their relationship beyond a momentary experience. Fantastic as it might be. And it had contained an element of love, a kind of fantasy love a child dreamed about, but adults learned could seldom be truly discovered. Realty was harsh; mean, cruel. Life lacked selfless love.

She hated that!

She hated what she was being forced to do with Greg.

She felt like a wanton of betrayal, a woman selling her body on demand and selling out her lover. All demanded by a husband who was nothing more than a business deal. A part of her hated him. But a deal was a deal. And they were in the thing together.

What had happened the night before had left her jittery, confused about herself and her life. "It's going to take time. I'm sorry. You can tell your damned Fat Man that it'll take time—and if he can't wait..."

"Delano is depending on us. You'll just have to hurry. Either you get the information we want—or

Greg Hern finds himself in a real scandal. If the newspapers found out about his playing around with another man's wife—I don't think it would look so good for him. He has to sign that contract! All you have to find out is if he plans on doing it or not. Do they need to use muscle to force him into line or..."

"Okay—I'll try. It'll just take time.... I have to go slow and careful. If he even slightly suspected something it would be—quite impossible!"

"When do you see him again?"

"Tomorrow night. At the same place," she said in a small voice.

"Okay—you question him—anyway you can. I'll have a recorder hidden. Voice activated. Afterwards make sure he makes love to you—and that there's no question about what's happening. We might need the recording to convince him to sign the contract."

There was an awkward silence and then Carl Bedford said, almost to himself: "I'd sure like to know why Delano's so all-fired interested in Hern."

Then without another word he stood and left the room.

Linda sat quietly for a long time, trying to settle the guilt wedged deep in her mind.

Greg had become an important part of her thoughts—and not in the way that Carl or Delano would have guessed, or liked if they had known. She had never known a man who had such an instant attraction for her. It was almost magical in a frightening way. He had made her feel important to him. It seemed as if he had been searching for her and found her, at last. Why should she feel that way? Black magic which had no place in her world.

It was romantic school-girl stuff. She had survived and managed pretty well, all things considering. All she'd had was a great body and the smarts to make good use of it. The marriage was the payoff. And being offered-up as a sexual toy for a man like Greg Hern was part of the price she was required to pay.

She felt dirty for the first time in years. And at the same time joyful at the idea of seeing this lovely wonderful man again.

Linda sighed, tired. Tired of life and tired of herself. She'd married Carl in the effort to gain position and money. Instead, it had turned out to be even a worse trap than the one she'd been running away from. Maybe that was why she believed that Greg was searching, because she'd been vainly searching for something she'd never been able to find. Maybe she was only projecting her own feelings on the man who had become an amazing focus, a wonderful experience, a...

She fought down those thoughts.

You're being foolish! She told herself.

Perhaps it was nothing but romantic illusion. And then, maybe something else. They were both alike in some mysterious way. From different worlds, yet they had connected with such a fantastic fiery force, fusing them together at some basic level that it was overwhelming.

Maybe that was why she loved him.

Bitterness went cold inside Linda. She tried to break her thoughts away from Greg Hern, because he was the man she made a promise to betray, and there wasn't any way of getting out of it, for a man like Fats Delano might do anything if crossed—she doubted he would stop short of murder. That was her husband's simple implication, warning. Don't cross Delano!

It was a long time before Linda went into the playroom where a cupboard bar was located. A drink was the only escape she'd ever been able to find that really worked. A long, long drink that didn't end until it had covered over all thought and all consciousness.

She reached for the first drink—it was a long time before the liquor clouded over her guilt.

* * * * * * *

Greg had followed his host into the man's den to discover a third man waiting for them.

He was a small, nervous looking man standing in the middle of the room. He turned and faced Greg. His white hair was messed as if he had been sleeping on a plane.

Judson introduced Greg.

"This is Henry Turner—he just flew in from the Orient; from my office there. Has something to report—something to tell you." Judson nodded to the other man. "Go ahead, tell him what you told me."

Henry Turner lifted his small eyes in Greg's direction and then after brushing his thin hair back with shaking fingers, he said: "This whole thing is bigger than we could have guessed."

He paused.

Greg asked: "What?"

"I just discovered that heroin is being shipped with Renton products. Naturally, our office in Hong Kong didn't know anything about it until the other day. I was just arranging things to come here to help out with the merger when I got word about it. Mr. Judson had wired me to look into the matter—when he found out about Delano being connected with Renton." The man paused a moment and then said: "And I smell…Arab connections with Delano."

Greg nodded thoughtfully. "Everything is connected. The Arab world is, of course, a part of international trade. That doesn't mean, necessarily, something bad. Not all Arab's are connected with Al-Qaida. That's just one group, world wide, sure, but percentage-wise, we can't paint all Muslims with the same brush."

"Usama bin Laden isn't small—"

"No, and he represents a very dangerous movement. Only one of many. But percentage-wise…the Muslim world is *not* inhabited solely by lunatics and fanatics. They're full of decent, reasonable people just trying to live their lives."

"He's right," Judson quickly stated in a rather nervous voice.

Turner said: "I know what this contract means to both of you, especially you Mr. Judson."

"I blow to Mr. Hern on this matter. He has better connections."

"None of us can know," Greg stated, eyes moving from one man to the other. "We can only make educated guesses. After what just took place in London—well…"

"Yes, yes, see what I mean? It is dangerous." the nervous Henry Turner stated. "What are we going to do about it?"

"Sit tight," Greg instructed. "The merger can be worked out. The Renton contract will take care of itself. As I understand it, we have a few weeks yet before the deadline. I take it they import to the US through Renton and then through Judson's company to mine."

The two men stared at him with open amazement showing in their eyes.

"How'd you know that?" Judson asked.

"I have my own ways. Just say most of it's guesswork. If the contract isn't signed with Renton a lot of business will be shot down the gutter, and John's firm folds. I know you depend a lot on Renton's business to keep you going, John, and that's why we have to be damned careful. It won't hurt me too much because Hern Industries does more than just importing and exporting. But I'm concerned about this as much as you are. Nobody here, I assume, wants to be supporting terrorist, directly or indirectly. We just have to take things easy. Getting excited won't help any. The only thing is that this has to be cleared up. We can't get involved with anything connected to terrorism. Possibly Renton doesn't even know anything about it. But don't blabber all over the place. Keep it between the three of us."

Turner was wide-eyed: "We have to do something!"

"We will."

"Don't you care?" Turner demanded. "I'm terrified. I didn't know if we should report to the authorities or not."

"You did right. I'm damned scared, too... I don't want to be connected with anything like heroin. But there are ways to take care of such matters." Greg was thoughtful for a moment and then, making a quick decision, said: "I'm going back to the States for a few days to look into this thing from that end."

"What about Delano?" Judson wanted to know, his eyes narrowing.

"We'll handle matters as they come up. I should return in a couple of days—but if not—I'll send a man to take care of the merger. I'm afraid the vacationing is over."

Greg turned and walked from the room, starting for the stairs that led to his bedroom. He had some packing to do and then his plan to disappear would go into effect. There was the seaplane waiting where he'd landed at Judson's ocean dock.

It was time that he made his first move against Delano.

He was almost finished packing when there was a timid knock at the door.

Greg paused and then asked, "Yes, who is it?"

"Carol."

He wanted to tell her to go away, then reconsidered, said: "Come on in."

The door opened and then Carol stepped up to him, closing the door behind her. "Dad said you'd be leaving. When will you be back?"

For a moment Greg stared at the young woman, a strange pang settling down over him. She had such an innocent and appealing look about her in those large sad eyes—and yet she was so savagely demanding, so blasted forward. In reality a spoiled little brat—even if a young woman in desperate heat.

"I don't know. I have things to take care of."

"You can't just run off like this. Can you?" she desperately choked out. The expression in her eyes held deep frustration and desire. "I won't see you again—will I?"

Sudden tenderness welled through Greg. Without even thinking he pulled her into his arms. It was an impulsive action, one which came from an inner desire to be gentle to a young childish woman. Breathing hard he slowly, gently moved her back.

Carol smiled up at him in silence for a moment, then said: "Couldn't we...go someplace? Before you leave? Now?"

For a moment Greg stared at her in amazement. She was a most unpredictable woman; there wasn't any way of knowing what could come from those beautiful, innocent looking lips.

Helplessly he considered. She was so lovely and so anxious to have him make love to her. If she were any other woman there would be little question as to what would happen. Perhaps he was making too much out of it. What could really be wrong with making love to her? What in the world could go wrong? She was a mature woman, demanding, and hungry for a man. Young and vital.

"I'll be good—you'll see. Believe me I'm good," Carol told him, pleading unashamed. At her age sex was either a very intimate, meaningful thing, or something experimental and casual. Either way she wanted to dive in almost blindly. But it was all wrong because it was not love, but pure animal passion. He didn't want to use her.

And after Linda.

Thought of her sent a dizzy gut level blow into him.

"Oh, Greg, I truly, honestly, want you—and I know you want me. I know the way you caress me with your eyes. What can be the harm. We're adults. I'm being boldly frank. I don't want to play games.

68

I don't want you to leave without having...at least once, known what it is like in your arms. Don't leave me wondering, and never knowing the truth. I'm very good. I know how to please a man. I just want to know how it is with you! The famous Greg Hern. I've wanted to know even when I was a virgin. But as an experienced woman...I really...want to know you in that way! Please! Please just this once! I won't demand anything from you...honest! No strings. Just let me have you this one time!"

Take her and be damned! he thought, both annoyed and pleased by the idea.

He wasn't in that much of a rush. And there wasn't any real way of knowing when he would return. And there was an outside chance that in the future something might happen to make the impossible. The time was right. Now or never. He'd always sought out a woman before facing the dangers of the unknown—he'd always tried to have that one more perfection of sexual union, whether it was purely physical or something more.

And after Linda the night before, and all that had involved, he needed to wash her out of his mind. If only she wasn't married. If only...

He mentally cursed at that.

But here was Carol, begging to be taken into his arms.

And who knew what might happen in the next days! Carol wanted him so much, if for no other reason except the fact that she'd stripped her emotions bare to him in her honest desire to become his. Even if for just a moment.

"Please, Greg..." she pleaded, lips just under his, so close he could feel her warm breath.

He swept her into his arms. Their bodies blended furiously together. She surged against him, wantonly. Her lips lifted and parted, and for a delicious moment met his. He thrilled to the surging thrust of her tongue as it searched for his.

He knew there was no backing out, now.

She was a fully matured woman. Young. Yes. But he'd bedded a lot of young woman. And she was blunt about her desire for him in such a manner few women were willing to so openly admit to.

Her kiss left no question in his mind that she was hardly a virgin.

He simply said, "The seaplane...that's the best place."

He finished packing and they left together.

The seaplane was small, but had a little cabin compartment in the back, just big enough to convert seats into a bed. It had been built for both business and pleasure to his own specifications. A playboy's dream.

Once the two of them were alone, Greg was amazed how quickly Carol came into his arms, as if some sultry devil possessed her, some demanding fire that had to be quickly consumed; some desperation that couldn't be fulfilled without the immediate union of their bodies.

He had expected an awkward buildup; a light conversation that would lead to the first kiss. He'd expected many things, other than what happened.

But instead she swiftly stripped without a word. Her eyes flashed in pleasure as he admired her body.

"You like?" she asked, touching her breasts, lifting them in the palms of her hands. "I think you like," she giggled in pleasure. "Now get naked, too. I want something to look at. To feel. To experience. I want you so much. I've dreamed of this for so long…"

She slipped close to him, before he could even move. Her hands lowered and came between his legs, exploring. "Oh, man, you sure are…super!"

He never really knew how he ended up undressed. Her hands were all over him, very aggressively searching, discovering, skillfully proving how experienced a young woman she was.

"Oh, Greg," she murmured, "I just love the way you feel!"

Then they were locked hungrily together, totally naked. Things blurred. At one point she was under him, soft, yielding, smothering his lips against her full breasts. Then she was on top, brazenly inserting him into her, enveloping him with the hot warmth of her flesh, sobbing, crying out in total ecstasy, clawing at him, giggling, gasping in turn.

"Oh, God!" she screamed out in joy when she had him totally captured. "You're…oh, Greg!"

Her body was surging up and down, feasting on him like a savage beast.

Carol was amazingly aggressive, not letting up once. A total unexpectedly fury of passion, driving at him over and over without stop. They parted several times, almost exhausted, then her caresses, lips, body took him with such demanding force that he could only respond.

It continued until she had totally exhausted Greg and herself. Only then did she fold into his arms, contented, sighing happily.

* * * * * * *

It was almost dark by the time he was flying high over the South Pacific, toward the island named Bikint, the place he had heard was Fats Delano's island headquarters.

The vision of Carol, as she had left the seaplane, child-like and so feminine, seemed like a distorted lie to what she had been in his arms. A wildcat, without restraint, an amazingly aggressive young woman who literally devoured her lover with almost mad passion.

He couldn't help vaguely wondering what had made her like that; what inner lusts could have driven her into being such a wanton. They were in many ways very much alike. Children of rich men.

Then his thoughts finally drifted to the under-cover work which the immediate future held for him. He forgot all about Carol, all about Linda, all about women and the light social life that he never tried to hide from the world; the social playboy's life had been his cover-up, hiding his true activities from the rest of the world.

Then slowly in the distance, Agent Green, alias Greg Hern, saw Bikint rising on the horizon

CHAPTER SIX

It was one of those cheap rooms, in a cheap hotel. The air itself was stuffed with the vile stink of age. There was a small bulb hanging from the ceiling and its dim light hardly reached throughout the room. The corners were still, darkened places where roaches made their homes. The bed, a board on legs, was infested with fleas and ticks.

Greg lay on the bed, already getting used to the lumpy hardness of the overused mattress. His mind wasn't concerned about how many whores had brought their clients up to this bed and allowed themselves to be used for a small price. One portion of his mind was aware that this was a place for such women. But he ignored this. In the late hours of the night the paper thin walls had sounded with murmuring voices and the crude laughter that blended and mingled and finally faded out for the gruff grunts of men hammering at the bodies of such whores. But this was also a place for bums and adventurers and seamen; a place where they stayed out the lonely nights—many with their tavern girls, some by themselves and their thoughts.

He was a bum, right now, he decided, already sick of his own body stench. The crying need for a bath was only argued down because of the need to appear as much a part of the surrounding island world as possible. He wanted to look and smell as if he had lived in filth and sweat all his life. It was part of the role.

A three day beard showed on his face, hiding the cleanly even, intelligent features—only his eyes revealed anything beyond hopelessness, for if anybody looked hard enough they would see a sharp intelligence that wasn't native to the kind of man he wanted people to see. He wanted them to hardly notice him and when they did, merely think he was another island bum.

For three days he had been on Bikint Island, attracting as little attention as possible, keeping his eyes and ears alert for information about the Fat Man.

Last night had scored what he'd been waiting to hear.

In a small harbor coffee shop, he had learned that the Fat Man was on the far side of Bikint; but was due to meet a yacht that was expected a little after ten the next morning.

Now it was up to him to connect himself with the man; get a job so that he could take the first step toward getting near Fats Delano.

Orders had come from the States that afternoon telling him it was vitally important to push, because Delano was expected to move a shipment of heroin through Renton, and much sooner than they had believed he would. This was his chance to possibly set a trap and smother the activities sooner than believed possible.

It was Agent Green's job to somehow put that

cleaver into the smuggling machinery and stop the shipment, anyway he could. And thusly stall the profits that would, in the end, be delivered to terrorist.

He lay there thinking for a long time in the semi-darkness, smoking one cigarette after another. There wasn't anything he could do right now, and until he could move, the only thing left was rest—he would need it.

Yet rest was slow in coming. Instead, his mind was traveling into the past, remembering, as it always did at times like these, how he had gotten into the Special Service and become Agent Green. A rather melodramatic title, job, position, and dedication.

But he had been doing this for a long time before 9/11 shocked the world into facing the very real threat of international terrorism. Since taking over the running of *Hern Industries* it was important to be especially alert to terrorist connections. Import and export business were on opening across national borders. Drugs converted to cash could be used to purchase weapons, people, and connections. The need to plant human cargoes into countries that had been determined to be targeted for terrorist attack was a prime focus of the fanatic hate-mongers. Their human-time bombs were too many times really just young kids without any real sophistication concerning western culture.

Greg understood the reasons for the hatred of western cultural influence. The propaganda basically painted all social imperfections as the direct result of the evil western devils. And, to some extend, their complaints seemed quite reasonable to them. The have-nots of the world always craved what the haves had. The weak desired power. And, sadly, power always perverted and the weak remained on the lower end of the social scale, desperately hungry for survival. They were told half-lies and then used like dumb beasts by a few strong, aggressive, many times uncaring men. The masters controlled the masses with an iron hand.

The cultural difference between the terrorist worlds and his were so black and white that it all too easy to convert basically illiterate people to believe anything that promised a better life. The promises were, sadly, empty. For in reality there were just so many riches in the world and the greedy could never get enough, at the expense of the weak.

It had never changed much, until recently. During the Cold War it had been a balancing act. Now it was madness. International communications, the Internet, mass media reaching around the world, made it all too easy to influence people, to pervert their personal worlds. And to organize international webs that appealed to the desperately frustrated poor. Anybody with a means to get enough explosives to turn themselves into human-bombs could cause serious damage. An organized mass of such people, financed by truly fanatic madmen, could very well, in time, bring down modern civilization if they couldn't be weeded out, stopped.

And when it was done in the name of the "local god"—no matter what it was called—then it became blind belief in a system that must rule, must win, must dominate in order to justify itself very existence. There was no room for rational compromise with such blind believers. And all sides had them screaming their concept of Truth for all to hear.

Greg even wondered if the terrorist could be stopped. It was possible that all that men like himself could do was slow their progress long enough for smart, reasonable people to resolved some of the very real problems that split such cultures into two mutually hating-camps out to destroy one another. It was a dim hope; but the only one left to cling to.

* * * * * * *

The sun was creeping over the horizon when Greg got up. He was dressed in worn jeans and an old T-shirt when he stepped from the hotel and moved down the small, narrow street.

There weren't many people up at this hour; the streets were just beginning to come alive.

There was a pleasant peacefulness to the island that contrasted violently from that of the big city life or the expansive, rich plantation existence on Temming. It was the kind of life that could appeal to him if it wasn't for his responsibilities; if he were to retire and seek the relaxed easy life that could have been possible. But that was denied because of his inner conviction that he had to live up to his heritage, and his choice of being a warrior against the evil forces that would ruin modern civilization.

It was only a few minutes walk to the small dock area of Bikint, and there he stood near the little fisherman's harbor.

Most of the boats were already out to sea beginning their daily work of gathering fish to be marketed. The men who manned them lived off their daily catch. It was a difficult existence, and he couldn't help admiring their guts. Not that they ha had choice; it was their only way to survive. He had been born to wealth. His own life had been totally different—and only through experiences as Agent Green had he really discovered how difficult it could be for the rest of the world. He'd been lucky.

He pulled out a cigarette. There were a couple of men standing near the railing that overlooked the blue waters of the Pacific. They had sweaty bodies and the clothing they wore was dirty and wrinkled, as if they had slept in them for days.

Greg felt the first pangs of hunger grind through him and walked off the dock towards the small coffee shop that served a crude black brew and hard bread.

Stepping into the dingy shop, he sat at the counter and ordered coffee.

The heavy woman that handed him the cup filled with the strongly odored drink grinned toothlessly and said: "How's things, Charlie?"

"Can't complain," Greg answered. Then he asked: "You're sure about this job?"

His eyes bore into the woman's lined face

"Charlie—he'll be here. I'll see about getting you that job. I know somebody that works for Mr. Jakes: You stick with me. I'll fix you up."

"Thanks," he grunted, taking a big gulp of the steaming coffee. It was terribly bitter tasting, but it jarred his mind awake, melting the sleepy numbness away.

He'd been in the coffee shop every morning, spending most of the day there so that he could learn the filtered island gossip. At night he had wandered over to the saloon which was the hangout

78

for the men in this section of Bikint. But it was here in this café that he learned about Fats Delano.

Like Temming Island, very little happened that everybody didn't learn sooner or later. A newcomer such as Delano couldn't go unnoticed for long—and rumors spread quickly through all social levels, finding their way to every islander.

He sat there until a little after ten, when a car pulled up to the dock and a huge fat man labored out of it.

Greg turned to the woman behind the counter.

"That the man?" There wasn't any doubt in his mind that this was Fats Delano—but he had to draw her attention to the fact of the man's arrival.

She stared out the window and after a few moments nodded. "That's him, Charlie. Danny'll be in for some coffee in a while—I'll talk to him."

Greg waited and then a small pickup pulled up in front of the coffee shop and several islanders and a couple of white men jumped off the back of it. They came quickly inside and ordered coffee.

It was several minutes before the old woman talked in whispered tones to a tall, hard-faced white man. After a moment he stepped over to Greg.

"I hear you want a job!" the man stated in a high grating voice. His eyes were like frozen stone, hard, cold, unemotional.

"I hear you need some help." Greg countered in a polite but firm voice.

They stared at each other for a short time and then the man smiled a hard, nasty grin. It had the quality of snake oil. "What you do?"

"Anything, just so that it's paying money. Don't care much what kind of work—doesn't matter."

79

The man squinted and then nodded. "Okay, get your things. I'll see you work. Five dollars a week, room and board."

"That's pretty cheap for a white man, don't you think, Danny?"

The man glared at him and then snarled: "Maybe if you turn out okay you'll get other work that'll pay extra. We'll see!"

He paused and said a little nastily, "Call me Mister Danny!"

"Okay, Mister Danny," Greg grinned, extending his hand toward him.

Mister Danny ignored it. He turned and walked a few feet down the counter. Without looking back, he called: "Meet me outside at the truck in fifteen minutes—that should be long enough to get your gear."

Greg paid for his coffee and went to the hotel. He was back in a few minutes, and waited outside, watching the car in which Fats Delano was sitting. When he heard the coffee shop door open behind him and the sound of voices, he turned to see Mister Danny approaching him.

"Well, let's get a move on, Charlie," the man demanded harshly, pushing him forward.

Greg shrugged and jumped into the car. They sat there waiting for orders.

CHAPTER SEVEN

The day's work was hard on Greg's muscles. They had been unloading crates from the large yacht onto the pickup. They were heavy crates marked "Toys." The urge to open one to discover, exactly, what they were was tempting; but quite impossible.

By mid-afternoon the work was over and they settled on top of the boxes as the truck started for the plantation on the far side of the island. Greg's muscles were tired. Even though he'd kept in condition all his life, actual labor came hard to him. The long drive managed to grate on his nerves, grinding them raw.

The island was covered by a mass of tropical jungle, unlike the copra of Temming. Bikint was largely a fishing settlement. Finally they came to the plantation and unloaded the boxes into a large building behind the bungalow.

Then they went into the bunkhouse where the hired help lived. Greg was assigned a bunk and locker. Placing his few belongings inside, he managed to keep the Army .45 hidden in a bundle of clothing. He didn't get a chance to pocket the automatic which would have made him feel more comfortable. In the middle of the enemy camp he needed the security of a weapon within an instant's reach. If anybody happened to see him and recognize his face as that of the famous Greg Hern, he wouldn't leave the island alive. That was always the risk he had to play out. Even with the beard they might see through his mild disguise.

His fellow workers were island men, anywhere from teenagers to past sixty. Most were friendly, but many quite, like himself, almost sullen.

Later, after having eaten in the workmen's hall, Greg lay on his bunk, waiting for the men to fall asleep. It was a long wait, for most of them didn't retire until late. By eleven, a dark silence had fallen over the bunkhouse, broken only by the light snoring of sleeping men

He waited a little longer

His mind was reviewing the day's events carefully, but there wasn't a hint that anything out of the ordinary had taken place—other than the fact that Delano had been a careful watcher over the activities. That was the only real clue that the shipment was important; and it didn't mean anything unless you knew the Fan Man's identity.

Finally he decided it was safe to leave. Carefully slipping off the bunk, he moved like a shadowy form across to the small doorway that led outside. There was a light creaking sound as he opened the door.

Greg froze. Intense anxiety flushed through him as he listened to be sure that nobody had heard him.

There was no indication that anybody had heard the door. After taking a silent breath of relief, he stepped out into the darkness.

The night air was sultry and the moon bright,

shadowing the world. Greg moved with the silence of a jungle cat, stepping from shadow to shadow toward the warehouse. He couldn't help wishing he'd been able to bring the gun with him, for if he were caught snooping there was a deadly chance he wouldn't see the sunrise in the morning.

His feet moved swiftly across the small clearing between the bunkhouse and the wooden building. About twenty yards to the left was the bungalow.

Greg's eyes kept shifting toward that direction, to be sure nobody stepped from the house unexpectedly and spotted him.

He was just about to slip into the dark shadow of the warehouse doorway when somebody stepped out of the bungalow, staring his way.

His guts tightened. Then casually he pulled out a pack of cigarettes and lighted one.

The figure spotted him and for a moment paused, staring carefully at him. It was feminine in shape and for several moments stood without moving. It wasn't until she was about six yards away that he recognized her.

For a moment, jarring shock numbed through him. He couldn't believe that his eyes weren't playing tricks on his mind.

Linda Bedford was stepping toward him.

He quickly turned away, slightly hunched over, so as not to be directly facing into the moonlight, hoping she wouldn't recognize him. It was a chance in a billion, and a dangerous one—but the only one he had.

Greg waited.

Linda paused for only a brief instant and then passed by. She hadn't recognized him.

He waited until she disappeared into the small garden that stretched out beyond the warehouse Then a sigh of relief rushed from his lips and he stepped to the warehouse door and placed a hand on the knob, twisting.

Disappointment flashed through him. The door was locked

For a moment he stood there in the shadowy darkness, and then decided.

Linda Bedford was here, and that meant that Carl Bedford would be here, too. Agent Baker had told him there might be some connection between Delano and the Bedford, so it added up. But what were they doing here?

He looked toward the house.

A window showed through into a large room, revealing several people moving beyond it. Greg made for it, carefully, silently. He stepped up to the window and then placed his head as close as possible, listening. Just as he decided it was impossible to hear anything, a rasping voice broke the silence.

"Just stay right there. Don't move, or you're a dead man, Charlie!" The voice was that of Mister Danny.

For a moment defeat iced through him. His mind jerked through several frantic thoughts: either he did something very fast or everything was blown. There wasn't any logical way of explaining his presence, and chances were that Danny would take him to Delano. In either case there was the chance he'd be meeting Carl Bedford and the man was sure to recognize him. He might be able to talk his way out of it with Delano—but once they discovered his real identity there would be no hope.

"Mister Danny, I—"

"Shut up and turn round slow. I have a gun pointed directly at your back. One move and it'll be the last."

Greg started to turn toward Danny; he moved slowly at first, and then without any warning he whipped around. This was his only chance—and he had to take it. One fast action.

He whipped to one side, hoping to avoid death while at the same time, in the same motion, rabbit-punched the man's neck. His other hand swung out for the gun. He twisted the weapon from Danny's numbed fingers and then smashed the barrel across his head.

For a second, breathing hard, he stood there over the unconscious man and then quickly stepped away from the bungalow.

His use on Bikint was all too quickly over. But he'd found something out that would make it possible to get one hell of a lot of information. Maybe through Linda Bedford he could get the rest of what he needed.

Greg slipped off into the darkness.

* * * * * * *

Linda Bedford had recognized the figure in the darkness. The intimacy they had shared had been such that she would have recognized him in any surroundings. The feelings his love-making had inspired within her had made his image a solid tender thing within her.

He was the first man she had really cared a damn for. The first to ever seem honestly truthful. If any other men had told her the things he'd said, it might not have been possible to even consider believing them. But Greg Hern had been telling the truth—revealing what he felt. At least for the moment.

What was he doing on Bikint was impossible for her to guess. His very presence there caused a mounting series of questions to spin wildly through her mind. *Why? What?* The impulse to rush up to him and feel his hard body against hers had been almost overwhelming.

He had recognized her; but remained silent about it. He didn't want her to know who he was. He was there for some purpose secret to himself. *But what? What could it be?*

So she had merely walked by.

Linda walked into the back garden, trying hard to hold down the inner confusion, the inner pain and agony.

She lighted a cigarette with shaking hands. Then standing in the darkness, she tried to weed out the chaos of her thoughts about her life and what it was she really felt for Greg Hern.

It was a long time before she decided to return to the bungalow and get some sleep.

When Linda stepped inside of the building she saw several people gathered outside the window of the living room. She heard their whispered voices, then recognized her husband. A terrible agony ripped through her.

They had discovered Greg!

She rushed forward and went to her husband.

"What happened?"

"Danny found the new hand snooping. Then the

86

guy slugged him," Carl Bedford explained. "Nothing to worry your little head about."

Relief settled through her, but she managed to keep her emotions to herself. *He had made it. There's nothing to worry about. He's safe!*

Then doubt bothered her.

"Where's the man?"

"He disappeared—but they're searching the area. He can't get very far."

"You better go into the house," Bedford continued. "We don't know what kind of crazy man this guy is."

Linda moved toward the bungalow, wondering what Greg Hern had actually been doing there.

That night she didn't sleep well because of her fear that they might find Greg. She didn't doubt the new hand had been Greg, or that Delano would not stop short of killing anybody that might get in his way.

The next morning Linda was relieved to discover they hadn't found him. In the afternoon she and her husband returned to Temming with the shipment of toys.

OPERATION: DOUBLE-CROSS, BY CHARLES NUETZEL

CHAPTER EIGHT

Greg's sudden return to the Judson plantation created quite a stir. Carol was delighted when she saw him. Once they were alone in his room, she drew him tightly into her arms, her lips covering his, trembling and moist. The kiss lasted only a few moments, and then Greg gently disengaged himself from the girl and started unpacking some of the things he had taken with him on the trip.

"I didn't expect you back so soon!" she breathed, gazing happily at him. There was a burning fire lighting her face. He knew what she was thinking, wanting; and couldn't help desiring the same thing.

"Is your father around?" he asked, after he had unpacked. They had been in his bedroom for a little over ten minutes.

"Can't that wait?" she inquired, disappointedly. "1 thought maybe now that you're back we might disappear some place for a few hours—you don't know how much I've thought about you."

"It's important, Carol," he explained gently. "I'm sorry. Business...well before..." He shrugged, tried to appear light and warm at the same time: "Before pleasure, you know."

"Damn you men!" Then she laughed. "Okay—he's in the den. Said to have you come to him when you were settled."

In five minutes Greg was standing before Judson, the den door bolted behind him.

"I have some information—I want to find out what you might know concerning it."

Judson's features were drawn. "Something about Delano?"

"And the Bedford, too."

Judson blinked for a moment as if he couldn't believe what Greg had said. Then finally he frowned, and managed in a thin voice, "What?"

"They're connected with this business—I'm sure of that. I couldn't find out anything more. And I can't tell you my source of information. You'll just have to take my word that I'm telling you the truth. The Bedfords were on Bikint Island. For all I know they still are—"

"They returned today. They were at Mr. Jake's plantation. A private birthday celebration. They're old friends!" Judson's voice filled with relief.

It was Greg's turn to be surprised. For a moment he just stood there, his mouth open, his guts churning. Then questions started to enter his mind; questions which weren't answered by Judson's statement.

"But a Mister Fats Delano is staying at the Jake's place, too. How's that fit together?"

For a long time Judson was silent and then said:

"I don't know!" His voice sounded puzzled, thoughtful. "But I'm sure of Carl Bedford. I've known him for years."

Then suddenly his eyes burned raw, firing savagely. Disgust shaded his voice as he yelled, "Wait a minute! Just because you're interested in Linda Bedford isn't reason to start slinging crap in their faces! I'm surprised. A little disappointed in you, Greg."

"John—for God's sake! You can't really think I'd do a thing like that, do you?"

Silence answered back. It was a chilled, cold, damning silence.

"This is a little too big for personal passions. And I don't think what goes on with a woman and myself is any damned business of yours. Linda isn't a child. I didn't even know she was married until you told me the other day. She was just a lady at the party—and she never told me her last name." Greg paused, taking a deep breath and then a thought jarred him.

"What a blasted egotistic fool I am! She must have been after me right from the start to pump information about the merger and the contract" He hesitated, and then continued. "That figures. All right, Delano must have found out we knew of his activities and wanted to know if we were renewing the contract."

"For what possible reason would he be interested in—" Judson broke off.

"I don't think it needs much explaining. Delano wants to make sure that everything continues to run smoothly, to keep his product moving through established channels. It'd be pretty messy for him to start all over again." Greg sighed. "I'll have to see Linda, in any case. I'd figured that this was possibly a good link—but now I'll be using it in a way I'd not thought of. Damn women anyway."

John was thoughtful for a moment and then said: "I can't believe Carl would have anything to do with a man like Delano. It doesn't seem possible! For what purpose?"

"Money?" Greg suggested. He didn't suggest anything else. He couldn't reveal the possible terrorists connections. That was something that only Agent Green would know.

"Maybe his being there at the same time was just an accident. How do you know? What right do we have to point a finger at—?"

"Don't be a fool!" Greg snapped, angrily. "I'm going over to find out. I'll pump Linda, for a change. But I need an excuse to make it logical. Linda will accept the fact that I want to just see her for—"

Greg cut himself short. "Damn it all! I'm not supposed to know she's married to Bedford. That fixes things up great!"

Greg thought frantically for a moment and then asked: "Can you send a runner over to her. I'll write a note."

"That won't—"

"It'll be all right," Greg assured him.

Judson thought and nodded. He said, grimly: "I hope you know what you're doing."

"I might be getting my neck chopped off—I'm betting with my own life!" Greg laughed nervously.

Ten minutes later a message was on its way to the Bedford.

* * * * * * *

Linda was sunning at the small pool in the

backyard when the native runner came up to her with the envelope from Greg Hern. She smiled at the young islander and then tore the envelope open, slowly unfolding the paper that had been enclosed. It read:

Dear Linda,

I know about you and Carl.
But I have to see you. Meet me on the beach outside your plantation—where we were that first evening. Come right away. I'll be waiting.

Greg

She sat there for a long time bathed in confused thoughts and worries. It was impossible to even consider telling her husband, regardless. The message, she realized, should be reported, but she wasn't going to. This was a private affair between herself and Greg. As far as Linda was concerned it wasn't anybody else's business.

The island boy was still standing there, waiting.

"Oh, you can go—thanks," she told him, smiling.

In a few minutes Linda started off the patio. She was able to slip out of the house unnoticed.

Greg arrived a few minutes before Linda. He was lying on the beach, enjoying the sun, and taking in the clear air. Temming seemed different from Bikint; there was a freshness about the place that was still clean and untouched by the scars of time. That, he realized, was partly his own personal state of mind It had been too close a call on Bikint

Suddenly, for a frightening moment, it had seemed hopelessly not worth it. His death would have gained nothing.

The muffled sound of footsteps shattered his thoughts.

"Hello," Linda's voice murmured as he turned.

It was like hearing soft music, like being caressed in the heart with gentle fingers. Again the magic of that first meeting and the magic of the second more intimate meeting flooded over Greg, drowning all other thoughts, all other reasons for living.

He looked up at Linda.

She was standing boldly over him, dressed in red shorts and an open white blouse that revealed the top of her white bra. The red hair flowed freely over her rounded creamy shoulders, and the light breeze made it look like rippling waves, floating gently.

For a long time there wasn't a word between them; only their eyes filled with meaning, communication and feeling. The thrill of the first night he had seen her, mixed with the intimate knowledge he'd learned later, sent needles of excitement over Greg. From the expression on her face she seemed to feel it too.

They were supposed to be working for opposite sides; they were supposed to be spying on each other. He didn't know how involved Linda was and she wasn't even aware he knew of her involvement. But all that didn't matter, for this was one of those strangely complex relationships that happened only once in a lifetime.

Suddenly they were in each other's arms, desperately clinging together, more in confusion than mere passion. Only after several moments did they pull back slightly, lips almost touching. For a few lingering seconds they merely looked into each other's eyes. Then slowly their lips closed the distance and touched and parted. The kiss lingered, first tender then passionately. Just as suddenly the embrace parted and she stepped back, away from him.

It was several minutes before either of them spoke.

Then she broke the silence.

"What were you doing on Bikint?" she accused, studying his face.

The question jarred Greg. It was some seconds before he could adjust to it after the impact of their embrace.

His guts were hammering and there was a sick webbing forming inside them. *She'd recognized him! And hadn't reported it—she hadn't told anybody!*

Joy mixed with confusion.

"Greg, I saw you—and what's more, you saw me. You know just as well as I do." Her voice was cutting and harsh, high pitched, but there was also confusion in her eyes. Hurt? Anger?

"So, I was there!" Greg found himself confessing and feeling a sense of guilt for not having admitted it right away. He realized it wasn't wise to tell her this, yet there was an inner relief at having done so. Plus there was, now, no way to avoid saying such things to this woman.

For a moment they were stone silent, listening to

the surf hammering on the beach. The sound of sea-gulls winging overhead made the conversation seem strangely out of place. This wasn't the setting for intrigue; for questioning or doubt; yet they couldn't avoid it.

Linda nodded, her face heavy with worry. "What were you doing there?"

"I can't tell you."

Linda slowly turned her face away and he could see that her full lips trembled.

"It's—a hell of a world!" she cursed in a choked voice. Her hands clutched into tight little fists. "Why do things have to be so damned compli-cated?"

"How?" Greg pushed, feeling it was the moment to grab this sudden advantage. For the first time he sensed that Linda was new at such intrigues; awk-ward and fumbling.

Or extremely experienced? he wondered.

"I—I started this…between us…as I was told to. Carl forced me. There's something going on here—and I don't like it!" she blurted.

Linda turned toward Greg, her face an agony of torment. "You don't know what it's like to have nothing! Nothing at all! Then some slob comes along and offers you everything! Carl Bedford wanted a wife for a front. A socially respectable front. Somebody he could be honest with—tell about his damned, dirty business. He's a god-damned bastard!" she stopped for breath and then hurriedly continued, as if scared that in a few mo-ments she wouldn't be able to continue; that she wouldn't have the strength to tell him what was so important for her to let Greg know. "At the time it

96

seemed the logical thing to do—now, I don't know. He told me to make a play for you—not let you know about my being married. The party was a perfect excuse—the moment he discovered you were at the Judsons' he made sure they brought you. I was supposed to pump you for information dealing with the Renton contract. And I didn't know you...then. How could I? I didn't know how we'd...how things would be between us. I just didn't know anything...damned!"

Linda hesitated and then choked out in a small voice that was trembling on the verge of teams: "I just don't understand it. I'm not made for such intrigues and...things like this. Oh, I've managed to make use of this!" She indicated her body, almost with contempt. "I sold it to a rich bastard. A business deal. But for a girl who came from nothing...to this...well, it was...a high-class sell. But not much better than a street prostitute."

"Hardly that," Greg suggested. "You did what you did to survive. Okay?"

"Not really. Yes. But...he got what he wanted I got what I wanted. A trade off."

"Business deal." Greg had known people involved in far nastier deals. He had seen the world from the rich down and exposed himself to the bottom levels of society and knew the difference. The rich enjoyed luxury which was made possible by the rest of society—off their sweat and lives. People struggled to simply survive from day to day. "I've seen far worse, Linda."

"No. I can't excuse myself that easily. But...this is where I am in my life, right now and...I don't want any part of it. I can't rationalize it all away.

I'm a…costly trinket in a rich man's hands…a toy doll to show off to the world. I'm a flashy jewel he uses to hide his dirty business deals behind. People see the glitter and none of the filth and dirt. And the fact remains I'm not much better than the local tramp, slut, selling herself for the price of a…I've known them. The junkie whores. And I've known a few higher priced ladies who sold themselves for hefty hard cash per night. Call girls. Call them what you will. And…"

"And you'd be surprise how much women sell themselves to men for status—or parents who arrange marriages with the proper male…business dealings. It is done all the time, on all levels of society. Some are called gold diggers, some are merely mating to their own social level, but most are, in one way or another struggling to connect to a person who will elevate them to a higher level—that old sayings: it is just as easy to fall for a rich guy as a poor one. Well, what's the difference?" he offered, almost tenderly.

"It is cold-blooded and…survival, I suppose—" Words broke off and she looked down at the sand.

Greg was silent for a long time before he asked:

"What do you know about a man named Fats Delano?"

Linda tensed. Her eyes flashed toward Greg. "Nothing, really. He's connected with Renton. So is Mr. Jakes. I only know they had some business together. The birthday party was an excuse—a cover."

She suddenly broke off. "Why the hell am I telling you this?"

Fear shaded over her features and for a moment she almost lost control of her emotions. Tears

98

welled and then faded. She lowered her eyes again.

But it was obvious why. Both of them realized that their relationship was far more meaningful than a mere one-night stand. Regardless of everything else, they were two people who had connected in a very real way. It happened.

"I don't know what they'd do if they learned I'd told you that," she whispered.

"They won't find out," Greg assured her.

For a moment the two of them were silent while the mood ebbed away. Then Greg stood, reaching for her. "Let's go someplace—to be alone!"

"The lodge," Linda suggested.

Ten minutes later they were closing the door of the large Bedford lodge behind them.

"Let's have a drink," Linda suggested, gliding over to the small bar in the corner of the room. She returned in a few moments with two glasses filled with amber liquid. "This is what we need."

They sat drinking and then after a little over ten minutes, Linda asked: "What are we going to do about—us?"

"We'll work something out. But one thing I promise, Linda. We aren't just going to let it end with a blank nothing."

They kissed gently and then finished their drinks.

"You really gave me a start on Bikint, Greg. That was the last place I'd have thought to find you."

"Let's not talk about it," Greg suggested. "Let's not talk at all," he added in a low, husky voice.

Linda slid down on the couch. Greg gazed into her eyes and saw the open burn of heat and desire beginning to smolder there and he knew it was time to move to her. Then they were finally locked together in the tight embrace of their bodies.

Greg felt emotions well up in him like a living thing, swelling every nerve and cell and hunger and need and affection until he thought he couldn't contain all of it at once.

It was then that he was willing to admit he had fallen in love with Linda; hopelessly and completely in love.

Whatever that meant!

CHAPTER NINE

They were sitting in the living room, alone. The Judsons had left for a visit with some friends, and Greg had only a short time ago returned from Linda. Carol sat in the large leather chair, her legs propped up on a footstool, her small hands clutching a brandy snifter. She was looking coldly at Greg, her face a study of pain that she made no attempt to hide.

"What'd you do today?" she demanded icily in a voice that revealed she had a pretty good idea.

Greg looked up startled.

"Call it business." He forced a smile, hoping she would leave it there. He didn't want to hurt her, but it might be necessary to do so. He couldn't help liking Carol, but that was as far as it could ever go. The relationship had been a mistake from the beginning. Carol wasn't mature enough to understand that—maybe it would take months or even years before she would realize that truth.

"I heard about your little message to Mrs. Linda Bedford," she accused nastily. Her voice was like stabbing ice. Her eyes narrowed, carefully watching for his reaction.

"If I told you there wasn't anything I could do

101

except see Linda—for business reasons—would you believe me?"

"Oh, for God's sake, Greg, what do you take me for?" Her words jabbed out at him in disgust. "I know the facts of life. Damn it all! You've just about given me every insult a woman can have given to her. Can't you at least be honest?" A long pause stilted the air, then she added: "It doesn't matter, does it?" She dropped her eyes to the brandy glass.

They were quiet again, and Greg let his eyes rest on Carol's young figure. It was as if some inner physical fascination possessed him; a desire his mind didn't want.

It couldn't be easy for her to know that after seducing him, he had gone to another woman—a married one at that. How could she help but wonder if this other, older, woman wasn't more desirable? That was a jolt that no woman would take unemotionally.

Greg didn't like hurting any woman. Especially one he had known for so long, one who was so young at that game. Being intimately involved with Carol had been a mistake, but one almost impossible to have avoided. She came on a man like a ton of bricks.

Carol sipped her brandy, all the time studying him. She didn't say anything. But there was an odd expression on her face, and for a moment Greg believed she was about to make some important statement. It was as if he were watching a novel being revealed on her features; the struggle was all subtlety, yet pitifully revealing.

Then she relaxed. "I guess there's nothing interesting on for tonight." The hope in her voice was painful to hear.

He didn't want to hurt her any more than necessary. Continuing the relationship would only scar her more, and that wasn't fair.

Greg sat there for several moments after Carol had gotten up and left the room. Her image faded in his mind, being replaced by another woman. He thought about the last words he and Linda had exchanged.

They had made arrangements to meet the next afternoon at the same place. The thought of seeing Linda again welled emotions through him, choking his throat momentarily. He'd never reacted to a woman like this before. It was a struggle to keep control.

Angrily he tried to push his thoughts away from Linda. He should be worrying about Hern Industries, about his assignment, not about a woman. Especially one he really hardly knew; a woman who had used her body to upgrade her social status in a very cold-bloodily businesslike manner. Yet, regardless of all that harsh reality, he could understand the necessities that had driven her—that would drive anybody to make the best deal in life they could at any given moment. Business was business.

Emotional complications could be damning. Why should a classy, good looking woman sell herself out to some local poor guy when she can have her pick of richer choices? Why shouldn't she make the best deal possible? And, apparently, the man who was now controlling her life had been, seemingly at the time, the best deal she had in the offering. Cold. Yes. But that was life on many levels of society. Everybody had a sell-out price. Even the very rich sold out to get better deals, more money, richer bank accounts, and larger international empires. Sometimes it was merely a matter of greed, mindless, uncontrolled hunger that could never to fully satisfied. How much was enough? What were the outer limits that any one empire might reach for? And, then, too, there was the horrid law that ruled everything: if you stood still you fell behind.

In business and in love.

And with Linda, Greg had found a woman who for some reason connected very powerfully with him. The why didn't matter: it was simply a fact.

What would be the end result? He didn't even want to consider that, for beyond the immediate moment it was a waiting game, with very little solid ground to support it. He was on that endless slippery slope. And like two people desperately out of control, he and Linda were clinging to one another in some very vital, emotionally deep way that went beyond logic, reason or even sanity. In its own way, that was survival on a totally different level—for both of them.

But the immediate moment was a waiting period. A breather; a pause.

Until Delano made his move, it was impossible for Greg to do much of anything. Still he had accomplished something this afternoon. Linda had promised to get as much information as possible on the shipment. She was now, from outward appearances, working on his side. But there was the always the chance that she'd been playing the smoothest game on record by convincing him she really was emotionally involved with him. She wouldn't have been the first woman to have fooled a man into a love delusion.

Irritated with his thoughts, Greg stood up and went to his room.

When he opened the door he saw a dark shadow moving in the room beyond. Tension tightened his gut and he quickly lunged forward, brutally knocking the figure onto the bed. Before he realized it, he was tangling in soft yielding flesh. His fingers merged with supple breasts and with a surprised grunt, he realized it was Carol struggling under him.

It wasn't the kind of situation a man could ignore or reject. Her lips covered his and a moan moved her chest.

Then the moistness of Carol's tongue moved along his lips, seeking entrance. He couldn't resist the invitation, and with a sigh of resignation he shifted his weight and drew her to him.

* * * * * * *

Later when Carol went to her room, bathed in the overwhelming joy of having again possessed Greg, she made a decision that was to change the course of her life and involve Greg in a mesh that would choke around him like a twining snake.

The next day she had to see Linda Bedford and tell her that Greg wasn't really interested in her— that he was just trying to use her. That would be the final seal in tying the knots around Greg Hern.

Carol realized it was a dirty trick—but there aren't any rules in love and war. Desperation had caused her to fight dirty before.

No matter what happened she was going to have Greg all for herself. She would win, no matter what it cost her. A little letter to Linda would fix everything.

* * * * * * *

When Greg awoke, a series of doubts plagued him. The last thing he remembered was rolling away from Carol's body, followed by nightmares that had ruined his rest. He felt as tired as when he'd gone to bed.

Showering and going downstairs to the breakfast room, he greeted the Judsons and nodded to Carol. He didn't like the eager, possessive expression on the young woman's face, but decided to ignore it by being completely impersonal.

They were halfway through the meal when a phone call came for him. Greg stood, excusing himself and then walked out into the hallway to the phone.

When he picked up the phone and heard the high nervous sound of Linda's voice, he knew something drastically was wrong.

"What happened?"

"I have to see you at once, but not at the lodge."

He heard Linda suck in a deep breath. "Delano's on Temming and—"

She broke off suddenly, then said in a different voice, controlled, unemotional, and impersonal: "And I hope that you won't mind meeting me at the market, later. Say about ten, Mary. I know you planned on shopping and I have a few things to get."

"Somebody there?" Greg asked.

"Why, Mary, how sweet of you to understand. You know I didn't want to cut into your plans. Look, I gotta go. Carl's here. I'll see you at ten, okay?"

"I'll be there—the market in town?"

"That's right."

The receiver went dead. His guts were tightened against his spine and he felt a mixed excitement. Delano was on Temming. Was he visiting the Bedford? More questions were mentally asked than answered.

For a moment he stood there thinking over the possibilities that this event suggested. Looking at his watch, he stepped into the breakfast room and motioned John to follow him. When they were outside on the patio he repeated what he'd just learned.

"What's it mean?" Judson wondered, frowning.

"Don't know—but maybe Linda can tell me. She was upset. Had to break off and act like she was talking to Mary. Her husband walked in on the conversation."

Greg stared at the other man and then, after a few seconds, forced a smile. "Well, let's finish our meal. I have until about nine-thirty. We don't want to keep the women waiting."

Judson attempted a smile, but failed. His face was white, drawn in lines of worry.

After a moment the two of them walked off the patio.

* * * * * * *

Linda turned casually and looked at her husband. There was a thin layer of cold sweat covering her body. For a moment it was impossible to say anything, but finally words formed.

"Hello, dear," she greeted softly.

Carl Bedford face was gray and his eyes squinted narrow, threateningly. For a moment he stood, staring, his lips drawn tightly across uneven teeth, his cheek twitching nervously.

"You better come with me," he commanded.

It was the strange sound of his words and the dead, frightened look in his leaden eyes that caused alarm to flutter through Linda. Something was terribly wrong, her mind warned.

The evening before he hadn't said much to her because there had been a lot of conversation with Delano. She had gone to bed early, more concerned about her feelings for Greg Hern than the fact that Delano was on Temming. It wasn't until morning that she realized Greg would want to know.

This was the first time she had seen her husband this morning. The man seemed somewhat annoyed, concerned, and even angry.

"What's wrong?" Linda tried to hide her own inner fears by an unconcerned sounding voice.

She smiled. It was a forced movement of her lips, drawing them tightly across even teeth.

"You'll find out." He gently motioned her out of the room. "In the study. Delano wants to talk to you."

They went through the house in silence and as she stepped into the small study, Linda was startled to see that there were a couple of men with Delano—men she had seen only at Mr. Jakes' place.

"Come here, Mrs. Bedford!" Delano ordered in a harsh voice. He nodded to her husband and the man closed and bolted the door behind him.

"What's going on?" Linda demanded in a much firmer voice than she thought possible to control.

Inner fear now generated through her. For the first time she felt the full impact of something very dangerous about to happen; something dangerous to her and possibly to Greg Hern. It was in the Fat Man's eyes; in the hardness of his thick, flabby face. Terror weighed down on her like a depressive hand which was attempting to claw away all restraint and control.

There was a long dead silence. Then Fats Delano stepped toward her. He stood in front of Linda for some time, his face chiseled ice; expressionless of emotion.

Without any warning his thick right hand lashed out across her face.

Linda felt her lungs contract, her throat choked dry. Her head was being torn to one side by the violence of the unexpected blow. She felt a salty taste in her mouth that was blood, and for a terrible moment her mind sunk into a deep well of terror, dazed and horrified.

The brutal hand slapped out again, whipping her head to the left.

Linda choked, rasping the pain away from her throat. Her arms raised in front of her face in an effort to protect it from another attack.

Finally she gained momentary control, gasping out: "What the hell? Why? Why?"

But some inner sense had already warned her what had happened. Somehow they had discovered she was playing on Greg's side now. They had managed the seemingly impossible.

"You little bitch, you should have known better than to try to double-cross me!" Fats Delano snapped. "I could kill you easily, without lifting a finger, without even giving instructions. Just you think about that!"

"What are you talking about?" Linda demanded, stepping back, shrinking away from him, and hoping to find some comfort from her husband. But there was very little coming from him.

Carl Bedford placed a gently protective arm around her for a brief moment and then tensed and jerked away. It was a meaningless gesture, and at the same time offered a subtle implication that nothing more could be expected from him. He would sit there in the room letting this man do whatever he wanted. Delano ruled totally.

Her mind reeled as she realized she was alone, trapped and helpless. They could kill her and Carl would do nothing.

His voice gave conviction to her fears.

"Don't try to get help from me, you two-timing little whore!" her husband snarled.

"What are you talking about?" she gasped out.

"We had the little lodge wired for sound, and the moment the door opened the recorder started. It was quite a little scene you played out. Swearing love and affection and trust and betrayal...we found it *very* interesting. We have a complete tape of what went on between the two of you." Delano icily told her. "I don't like a woman who switches sides. Do you think we're amateurs?"

Linda's mind quickly fell into another channel, desperately trying to search for an explanation they might accept. She hadn't survived in a real nasty

110

jungle as a child and young woman without having some honed skills. Now, automatically, they came into play as she retorted angrily:

"You stupid fools! What do you take me for? A complete idiot? I knew the setup. Carl told me. I've seen what's been going on and I'm not about to back out on you guys. You don't really believe I'd cross you? Or my husband who's given me so much?" She turned tender eyes toward Carl.

"We heard what we heard," Bedford told her in a coldly dead voice.

"That's what you think!" Linda managed to literally snarl, turning toward Delano. "You smart men. So cock-sure of yourself, and so high and mighty, ready to slit somebody's throat because you think you heard something that sounded like a double-cross." She laughed and then cursed, "You damned stupid fools! How dumb can you get!"

Her contempt was thick, and she stood straight, staring directly into the Fat Man's cold eyes.

"Maybe that's why we're listening instead of slitting your throat," Delano observed calmly, his eyes making a deep, probing study of hers. "Popping a bullet into your lovely head before dumping your body in some deep well or somewhere in the ocean can be done anytime we so decide. Maybe we might just have a little fun with you? Why waste such a lovely lady? Right, boys?" The man turned and looked at his henchmen, who grinned. "We could make you the local whore, in some room for our own pleasure—and your husband would do nothing to stop us. Right, Carl?" The man didn't wait for any response from him. "So...just understand, we own you, dead or alive!"

Hard silence waited for her answer.

"I had to say what I did. I had to make him think I was playing it on his side. You don't think he's a fool do you? You don't think he's about to open his heart to a woman he hardly knows, do you? It takes more than stripping a body naked, flaunting it in front of a man and letting him play with it. You don't think a man like Greg Hern is about to suddenly tell me his life's story and his business intrigues just because I'm throwing myself at him?" Stony silence answered her.

"I told Carl that Greg wasn't easy to pump. So what was I supposed to do? The only thing possible! I have to make him think I'm in love—so he'll believe me. Believe everything I tell him. I have to make him think I'm working on his side. Then—and only then—will he talk to me about what he plans to do."

"That's not good enough!" Delano snapped. "I don't believe you understand the situation.

"I've learned through some sources I have that Greg Hern is more than what he appears to be on the surface. It's rumored he's working for the United States Government: a Federal Agent. But I have to be sure—I have to know exactly what he plans on doing.

"I want to find out how much he knows about me. We're walking an international tightrope. We have a nice little thing going here, and there's no reason to kill it before we are certain we have to pull out. As far as I'm concerned, political matters, ethical matters and religious fanatics don't really interest me as long as they have hard cash to back up their needs. Somebody connected with the US government tossed in the mix is danger city to me. I don't need that. I have too many sweat deals in the makings. And I'm getting a bit nervous. Like I said, we have reason to believe he's working for the US of A, but we have to know for certain before making any drastic moves. If he's what we thought him to be...well, that's another matter.

"I don't want to crush the golden egg, so to speak. And Hern Industries is a magic road around the world and back. And a way to fatten our personal bank accounts. I'm hoping for the best. Without Hern we can survive, but it'll hurt. But hurt far more if he turns out to be one of those nasty bad guys working for some US of A...well, you can see what I mean. And this makes me nervous. Something I don't like. I'd much rather be calm and peaceful and enjoy the rich rewards of my daily duties at my floating office."

Delano shrugged, paused for a moment, studying Linda, and then continued: "There's a man that answers to the same description as Greg Hern who does work for the Special Services under the code name of Agent Green. Nobody of importance has come to the islands—and none with the description of Agent Green *except* your Mister Hern."

"And you want me to find out?" Linda asked, hiding the inner disgust that tightened nausea in her gut.

"That depends. As of right now I'm not really convinced you're on our side." Fats Delano lumbered away from Linda, and then nodded, waiting in silence.

For a moment she thought over what had been said; working with the different possibilities. What if Greg Hern was Agent Green, and knew about her husband's connection with Delano and had simply used her?

That possibility crumbled Linda's emotional world. Her whole life was up on the chopping block, cruelly being butchered by people who were merely using her for their own means—both sides toying with her emotions and her body. It was such an old story for her that she had hardly any emotional reaction. As long as Linda could remember it had been like that—people using her for their own means; without any thoughts about her as a human, feeling person.

Everyone was thinking about themselves, so there wasn't any reason she shouldn't do the same. Play both ends toward the middle, and then move to the winning side with honors and glory.

"I'm meeting Greg in the market at ten. He thinks I have information for him. He knows about you being on Temming. How, I don't know." She stared evenly at Delano, not flinching a muscle. "I was going to tell you that, but you didn't give me a chance."

This was a new game, a game she had to learn fast in order to survive.

The Fat Man gazed fishily at her and then pursing his heavy, thick lips, nodded. "Okay, I'll give you information to tell him—we'll set up a little trap and see what happens. And you better pray that things happen the right way—or you'll end up in the Pacific Ocean. Deep down where the fish don't swim!"

* * * * * * *

It was nine-twenty when Linda left the study, her mind sick, her body aching at what she was turning into. A few short hours before she'd thought she was in love with Greg Hern and that he loved her, and now she didn't know what to think.

Going to her room she changed into a flaring skirt of red cotton and a white blouse, much as the island women wore at the market place. She let her hair fall free and loose around her shoulders and then started down the steps to the front door.

A maid stopped her in the hallway. "This message came for you, Missus."

Her first reaction was to wonder why Greg would be writing her. Then as she tore the note open she recognized the handwriting as being feminine. She read:

Mrs. Bedford,

I thought it only fair to warn you that Greg Hern isn't interested in you and never has been. He's been playing for information.

It was unsigned.

She stood there, staring at the note, numbness making her dizzy. It could have been written by one of Delano's men. Yet it might be from an outsider.

Slowly she melted the tight knot inside her, fading away the choking emotions. Then she stepped out of the house and went to her car.

All the way into town, Linda was hating herself for the terrible trap she'd allowed her life to become. Her hard years of bumming in cheap bars and fighting for an existence was enough to make her realize that there was only one person worth saving and thinking about, and that was Number One— Linda! Nothing else had ever counted, and didn't count now or in the future.

CHAPTER TEN

The small marketplace was something out of another age and another world. Unlike the neat rows of manufactured canned goods, piled one on another, unlike the neatly wrapped lines of meats that were common to the modern supermarkets, this was a Mardi-Gras of native coloring, tented in bright reds, oranges, blues, greens, yellows. Native women clothed in crude skirts and blouses reached out chubby greased hands frantically attempting to sell their goods. There was a jagged line of open shops with island boys carrying their trinkets or fish or produce on their backs, stopping anybody that might pass. The flavor and aroma was a combination of fish, spices and sweat.

Greg made his way through the gathering crowds, searching for the familiar face and figure of Linda Bedford. The tropic sun had already made is presence known in a fiery blaze. His blood was pounding at top speed through his body. Sweat lined his forehead.

He'd arrived several minutes late and by the time he'd pushed and clawed his way through the milling crowds three times, he had given up hope. Looking at his watch, he saw it was 10:20, and no sign of Linda.

A gnawing fear brought on a cold ice down his spine.

Once more he would try to locate Linda, then he would take other action. What that might be, he couldn't imagine right then; but he'd think of something. If anything happened to her somebody was going to pay highly for it.

He'd gone through one last time and was about to return to where he'd parked the new car the Judsons had loaned him when he spotted a red head bobbing in the crowd. Relief pounded at his chest and he rushed forward.

It had to be Linda.

Then he saw her face and sped toward her. As they came together they stood silently gazing into one another's eyes.

He reached for her hands and gripped them affectionately. Neither of them said anything for a moment; once more the magical silence of their eyes said all that was necessary.

Then finally he smiled. "You gave me some scare. I've been flying through that market for twenty minutes looking for you."

Linda was serious as she said: "Something happened. I'm sorry."

"I don't know what I would have done. I'd just given up hope. Probably I'd have rushed into your home like the Lone Ranger, guns blazing, coming to the rescue of the young girl in danger."

This time Linda laughed, but it was nervous and high pitched.

"Something's wrong, isn't it?" he inquired, starting to lead the way to his car.

118

"Yes. I'll tell you later."

Her hand was hot in his, damp. But the contact melted all thoughts of international intrigue. All he wanted to do was disappear from the world and be with Linda. Nothing really seemed to matter when he was with her. Perhaps it was illusion, yet a very beautiful one.

They stepped up to the car and he helped Linda in. A moment later he was behind the wheel.

It seemed strange to Greg that this woman, whom he had only known for a few days, could have such a strong effect on him. In just a few days she had become so very important.

Greg started the car and pulled into the narrow Street.

"You know someplace?" he asked, turning toward her.

"The lodge is out."

"Where, then?"

"Just follow the road out of town and then at the first turn to the left...I'll show you when we get there."

They didn't say anything while he drove out of town, and only her directions broke the long silence after that.

They drove through green covered land, speckled with the brilliant colored flowers. This was not a setting for intrigue, but rather for love and romance; a place where lovers come to enjoy paradise.

But there wasn't any fooling himself, Greg admitted bitterly. He was now Agent Green—not Greg Hern, rich playboy. That illusion was gone; unnecessary at this time and place. Yet the woman sitting in the car with him wasn't just a nobody or a person he didn't care about. He cared too much. And therein lay the danger.

He must make Linda believe it was Greg, businessman, playboy, driving the car. She must believe that nothing else really mattered, that he was only concerned with business matters—and more importantly, only in the belief of their love for one another. This was a game of lies, based on deception and betrayal.

Finally Linda's directions led them to a small lake surrounded by tropical underbrush and multicolored flowers. This was paradise within a paradise.

They sat in the car for several minutes before Linda said anything.

"This is a lonely place except on Sundays. Then all hell breaks loose. The island boys and girls come up here to bathe. They laugh and play as if nothing else mattered in the world." She laughed nervously again and then sighed. "Not much of a setting for what we have to do, is it?"

She turned pleading eyes up to his.

Greg nodded and suggested they get out and take a walk.

"It's strange, Linda, that the world can't just roll over and die—leave us alone. A man could easily come to a place like this and forget everything that seems so important to the outside world."

Linda's voice sighed out, tiredly: "Maybe I know what you mean." Her hand squeezed his.

Then Linda's face took on a serious complexion. Her lips clamped tightly together for a moment and then abruptly said: "It's a damned world!" Harsh bitterness filled her voice. "Why can't we just

120

forget everything? Disappear. Leave all the slobs to sweat out their dirty little intrigues. What do they mean to us?"

For a moment they stared at one another, feeling the desperate loneliness, the terrible weight of pain that had been brought down on their lives. In this, if nothing else, they were as one.

Suddenly their lips were crushed tightly together, their bodies straining in the embrace.

Greg felt his body trembling.

It was with great effort that he forced his lips to ask the question: "What do you have to tell me?" It was soft and hesitant, but he wanted to get it over with, then throw it aside to be examined later when he had time for such matters. Right now he had only time for himself and Linda. That much the world owed him. At least he tried to offer that up as a rationalization, but it didn't work.

It was a few moments before Linda answered. Her face was drawn tight, her lips started to part, as if to say something, then she turned away.

She stood there, her arms clutched at her sides, her hands balled tightly, as if every nerve in her were fighting an inner struggle, an emotional battle.

"What's wrong?" Greg asked, emotion caught up in his voice.

"Nothing. Nothing at all!" she answered softly.

Greg stood for a moment and then placed gentle hands on her shoulders and swung her around to face him.

"Can't we talk about it a little later?" she pleaded in such a desperate voice that he felt extremely tender towards her.

"If it doesn't matter. You know how—"

"It's not that. It's about tonight. So maybe we could—could just be together for a few hours. Have each other and forget about all that—"

"Whatever you say, Linda." He took her hand in his and they started walking around the lake.

Finally they came to a small inlet of sand, surrounded by water. Greg led her toward the back of the inlet and they sat down holding hands. The simplicity of the act was complete in itself.

"Greg—why is it you're so interested in Delano?" Linda inquired.

"I can't tell you that," he said flatly.

Linda ignored his statement. "You know what kind of man Delano is?"

"Why?"

"Just tell me!" she demanded.

"That depends on what you are talking about," Greg countered, avoiding any confession.

Linda was silent for a brief moment and then shrugged her shoulders. "Just—I don't know. I don't like him. He's dangerous."

"What makes you think that?" Greg asked, innocently.

"I don't really know. Carl and Delano are involved in something. It has to do with a shipment they are sending to the States."

Greg felt tension weld his nerves tight. Outwardly he attempted to remain calm. "I understand he has something to do with Renton. That would seem only natural—wouldn't it?"

"I guess so," she admitted. Then her mood changed abruptly. She turned toward him, her eyes fearful, desperately pleading. For a moment she stared at him, her lips parted slightly. She moistened

122

them with the tip of her tongue.

"What is it you wanted to tell me?" Greg finally asked.

Linda worked her lower lip between her teeth and then slowly said: "Go to the lodge tonight—there's a shipment of heroin there. That's what I've learned—but...you'll have to check it out yourself, I guess. There won't be anybody there."

Greg was jarred by her blatant announcement. He hadn't realized she knew so much. It sounded like a nice little trap. All the way back to town Greg was spinning in a whirl of questions, none of which he could ask Linda. Not even Linda must know he was Agent Green. But what bothered him most was wondering if she might already know and that Delano knew and they had set a trap for him. It was only the memory of her lips, warm and tender against his, which shredded the warnings of a possible trap. For they had made love in the most gentle and meaningful way. It was simply a concert of beautiful touches, blending into caresses and kisses that finally united her body with his body in a splendor of love-making that left him exhausted and filled with joy. In each other's arms nothing else seemed to matter. When he gazed into her eyes it was as if they united into one total being. They had discovered one another's very spirits, uniting into one intermingling soul. That was the final argument which convinced him that he would be safe going to the lodge.

* * * * * * *

After Greg left her, Linda slipped into her car,

still dazed at what had happened and what she had done. Guilt made self-hate a pleasure. Everything she had done in the past seemed like water to a very red wine. The only man she had ever loved, the only one she would ever love, the only man who had been really decent to her, she had betrayed, setting him up for a trap from which he wouldn't return alive.

Her life as a prostitute had never been quite that low. Her marriage to Carl Bedford hadn't been as cheap and dirty.

The ride home was a study in agony and disgust. Yet, she reasoned, desperately trying to discover a rational excuse for her actions, what else could she have done?

Life was a cold struggle for survival and the victor won in any way possible. No hold barred, nor too degenerate or nasty. The winner survived. Nothing else mattered in the long run. You lived or you died.

When she arrived home, her husband was waiting for her. She stepped into the living room and he moved to her side, his face drawn tight, his cheek on the verge of twitching.

"What happened?" he demanded in his high voice.

"I did as I was told," was her only answer.

He nodded, studying her eyes.

Neither of them said anything for a long time. Then he nodded to the glass in his hands. "Want a drink?"

"Damned right!" she exploded.

She could use a lot of drinks, enough to get her completely smashed. That would be the only way to

124

face the next hour. The only possible way to escape her tormented thoughts.

"Where're the pig and his buddies?"

"At the lodge, waiting."

Panic weakened her insides and nausea threatened to empty the lining of her stomach. Linda clutched her hands, squeezing her eyes shut against the agony that ripped through her at Bedford's words.

Was Greg already dead?

A drink was in her hands and then she felt the burn of raw whiskey stab down her throat and settle like a fiery lump in her stomach. It ate its way through the nerves of her body.

"Linda," Bedford's voice cut into her thoughts.

She looked up at her husband, controlling the hate she felt for the man.

"What?" she managed in a small voice.

"I—I don't like this," he told her in a soft whisper. It almost sounded like a moan.

"A nice time to think about that. Why don't you do something about it, then?" she demanded nastily.

"I can't. You don't understand what kind of men we're dealing with. And anyway I'm a coward. I've known that for many years. I've always been a coward; I always will be one. That's what got me into this in the first place." He sounded half alive; his eyes were blindly looking at her, as if gazing into some distant past. "I was a young kid when I got connected with the Communists. I didn't realize what it was really all about. As an idealist and weak to boot, it seemed a way to get strong—belonging to something important. I didn't know—but that's past, now.

"And when the USSR crumbled, when...all of it changed.... It's a nightmare! They get their hands on you and you can't get away. You are choked by them, squeezed until there isn't anything to do but go along. You don't know who you are really dealing with, or whom they deal with...it's all mixed up and 9/11 and all that.... I don't like what's happening, but I can't change things. They beat all the fight out of you. Finally you get into a situation like this—and you're helpless."

He paused and then added, more emotionally:

"If it helps any, believe me, I love you, Linda. I didn't know how much until I heard that recording—what you had told Greg. I—I know you were speaking the truth. A man learns about his wife, he can't live with a woman very long without knowing when she's telling the truth and lying. You...."

Linda was amazed. "Why didn't you tell Delano?"

"I couldn't let him kill you, and he would have if I'd told him. I was helpless, praying you would find some way out—some way to convince him it was all a lie." After finishing his drink, he added:

"I hoped you wouldn't come back. I was hoping you would be—I'm sorry about all this. I—"

His voice broke off and then he sat down, looking at the far wall, his face a white blank of all emotions; his eyes dead, blind.

Linda finished her drink.

Greg would be going to the lodge—might be there right now. It would be only a matter of minutes before he was dead. If only she hadn't told him about it; if only she had told him the truth.

126

Her mind argued that no matter what she would do, it would be a gamble, and she might be playing with her own life.

But wasn't love more important than anything else?

Love had its responsibilities. How could she live, knowing that she'd sent the only man she loved to his death?

That decided the issue for her.

She left the living room and went into her husband's study. There was a gun in his desk drawer. She took it, checked to make sure it was loaded.

Hesitating for only a second, she rushed from the room.

OPERATION: DOUBLE-CROSS, BY CHARLES NUETZEL

CHAPTER ELEVEN

Greg drove directly to the Judsons' place and went to his room. There wasn't much time to play out his move. Everything he did from this moment on would be a calculated risk. It was a risk to believe Linda—to believe that she hadn't actually set him up for a trap. But the only way he could find out for sure was to investigate the lodge himself. To get the police involved at this time would mean to reveal his true identity—and possibly ruin his whole play. That was a gamble he wasn't willing to take.

He hadn't seen anybody in the house when he went through it and for that he was relieved. The last thing he wanted was conversation. But when he was checking the .38 he'd taken from Mister Danny on Bikint, footsteps startled him.

Greg whipped around. His first impulse was to hide the weapon, but it was already too late.

Carol was standing in the doorway looking at him.

"What's that for?" she asked, her eyes large with surprise.

He shrugged off the question, trying to act casual.

"It's a private matter."

Carol's face pinched and her lips seemed on the verge of trembling.

"What happened?" she blurted, rushing forward, stopping a few feet from him.

"Business. I don't have time to explain. It's private, anyway." He looked into her eyes, hoping she'd leave it there.

Carol stood staring at him for a moment and then rushed into his arms, circling his neck, covering his face with kisses, and hungrily pressing her body against his. "I love you—I love you, Greg. I don't want anything to happen to you. I love you!"

He felt embarrassment flush his face as he held her back. "Carol, don't be a child. Nothing's going to happen."

"I love you, Greg. I don't want anything to happen to you." Tears streamed down her throat.

"You don't love me, and you know it," he snapped cruelly. Now was the best time to end things once and for all between them.

"What are you talking about?" she gasped, stepping back, her face flushed red.

"That you don't love me," he said as gently as possible. "You're attracted to me—that much is painfully obvious. But it's nothing more. So—just don't get all worked up over nothing."

"I do love you," she cried out in desperation, as if trying to convince herself while convincing him.

"You think you love me. A woman your age falls in and out of love very fast. You're experimenting, that's all. You haven't learned the difference between passion and love."

"What do you know?" Carol spat out. "I want you—I've lied, cheated fought—I've done things

130

most women would cringe at doing, that most women don't have the guts to do in order to win their man. I'll do anything to have you!"

"Please, Carol. Do we have to have a scene?" Greg said in a tired voice.

"Yes, we do," she yelled, her face livid with emotion.

"You men—think you know everything," she laughed bitterly. "I'll do anything to have you. And I can prove it. Who do you think had you pushed around after you'd seen Linda? Her husband? Hell no! I had that done. I wanted you to stop seeing her. I did that because my love was so great that I'd do anything to possess you. I even wrote a note to Linda this morning saying you were only using her. It was about time you cleared your head about that slut." The sudden outburst stopped, as if Carol realized she'd said too much; or it might have been the expression which twisted Greg's face that stopped her.

Only with control was Greg able to keep from hitting her. She would have been the first woman he had hit. His muscles tensed and he felt his right hand start to move. Then he forced himself to freeze.

Suddenly Greg didn't feel anger for Carol; instead, he felt pity. It was desperately sad that a woman would go to such extremes for her own personal desires; desires that weren't anything more than a child's hunger to be wanted and needed. All for an emotional experiment.

"I'm sorry," he sighed. "There was never anything between us—and there never could be. Outside of friendship. It was a mistake from the begin-

131

ning. I should have known not to let it start. But blame my normal male desire for a beautiful woman, very desirable woman....you are a very attractive girl and will make a fine wife for some man—but wait a few years, learn something about the world and yourself before you lunge into something like marriage or love. Right now you're just in love with love, the idea of love."

Carol stared at him for a long time, her face a study of agony. Then without another word she turned and rushed from the room.

It took him about ten minutes to drive to the Bedfords' lodge. During the ride his mind was carefully working over the possible turn the next few minutes could take.

Even though it seemed impossible to believe that Linda had been putting on an act, he might be walking right into a trap. Linda was married to Bedford, who was involved up to his ears with Delano. She might be a very clever actress. Many agents had been killed because they had trusted a woman with whom they believed themselves in love. It was an old trick and the people he opposed were professionals in intrigue. They believed the ends justified the means and could be very cold-blooded about it. And religious fanatics were more than dangerous. When one was an extension of God's will on Earth, then anything was justified in the name of The Cause. And Delano was, without question, even far beyond that: a dangerous, self-centered power player, who would squash anything that got in his way, without even a flicker of guilt. He believed in nothing beyond his own personal needs.

Finally the car turned the last bend and the small

lodge came into full view.

Greg pulled the car to the end of the road and then got out. A last-minute check of the gun and then he put it into his coat pocket.

The lodge was dark and silent, waiting like a vulture about to spring into attack on a dying man. The quiet might be a dangerous deception. Greg put his hand inside his pocket, feeling the cold metal of the automatic, as he stepped onto the front porch. He took the key from under the door mat, fitted it into the lock and turned it. A moment later he stepped into the darkened house.

No sound met his ears and he momentarily relaxed, reaching for the light switch.

The darkness exploded into light as Greg turned and looked into the room.

"Hello, Mr. Hern. How nice to meet you at last. We've been waiting for you!" A huge fat man greeted. He was sitting on the couch that faced Greg.

"Don't try anything, *Charlie*," a familiar voice ordered from his left.

Greg turned his eyes to see the form of Mister Danny, the Jakes' foreman.

"Well, I see everybody is here. How nice!" Greg observed, forcing his muscles to relax against their will.

There was a stony silence and then Fats Delano smiled like a reptile.

"I'm glad you were able to come. It makes things real cozy to know that everybody comes to the party. Makes you think you're popular. Quite frankly, I like being popular. In fact I just love it!" He stood and motioned Greg forward with a jerk of

133

his beefy hand. "Have a seat. Please. Be comfortable."

Greg didn't move.

"Do as the Boss says!" Mr. Danny ordered, jerking forward and pushing the .38 revolver into Greg's side.

Delano said in a soft voice: "Now, now Mr. Hern. I insist that you simply sit down…like a nice man!"

Greg tensed and then slowly stepped toward the Delano, never moving his eyes from the Fat Man.

"Sit down, Mr. Hern," Delano offered in a friendly voice. "There's no need to be formal about this. After all, aren't we friends? Well, okay. We're supposed to be friends. And that's all that counts."

Greg sat on the sofa and looked around him. There was a third man standing in the background, a revolver in his hands.

"I see you brought a couple of goons. I wouldn't think a big man like you would need help!" Greg observed nastily.

"You never can tell." Delano's expression never changed from the polite formality. His fat features were still grinning, his beady eyes narrowed, staring probingly into Greg's.

"It's your party, Mr. Delano."

"You know my name?" The man was honestly surprised, slightly pleased at the revelation. "How wonderful. Now that really makes me feel liked. I'm famous. Apparently. How lovely. So nice to be not only popular but famous."

"I thought everybody knew your name. I thought you were a household word for bastard!" Greg's eyes were centered on the bridge of the

134

man's nose. He didn't flinch. This was a game both of them knew well, a game of sizing up, of judging each other. It was almost like a corny recreation of some old film such as *The Maltese Falcon* or *Casablanca* with Sydney Greenstreet playing off against Bogart. Only this was real life. And Delano didn't have the winning charm of that character actor.

Danny started to jerk forward at Greg's insult, but Delano waved him away.

"I'd really like to know exactly what brought you here this evening, Hern," Delano inquired, unconcerned, as if above all kinds of insults.

"I thought you knew that. You're so well informed. Your little spy was very good—quite experienced and professional. Extend my compliments. I fell right into your trap like a little innocent child."

"I wouldn't call it a trap. I just saw to it she invited you here. That's all." The smile was still on his face, but hardness set his eyes.

A cold sweat broke out over Greg's body, and he found himself wanting to reach into his pocket and get the whole thing over with fast. There wasn't any way out of this situation; that much he knew. Agent Baker had warned him that it wouldn't be possible to help him if he got caught. Now he was painfully on his own, against three men who would think nothing of killing him.

"Okay, now. Let's cut the crap!" Delano snarled. "I want to know what your interest is in this thing. And now!"

"I might ask the same question," Greg countered.

"Don't be funny." Delano nodded his head toward Danny and the man stepped up to Greg, tense and ready, a sadistic grin spreading his face. Delano said: "You had better make things easy on yourself."

"Go to hell!"

Danny's hand slapped brutally across Greg's face. It was a stinging blow. The salty taste of blood oozed into his mouth.

"You don't want to be forced into giving us the information we want, do you?" Delano inquired in a silky voice. "It would be a pleasure for Danny—and you wouldn't want that, would you? I'm sure you don't want to give him all that pleasure! At your expense."

Danny's hand lashed out again. This time a hard ring cut a gash into Greg's cheek.

He sat there dazed for a moment, his thoughts muddled. It wasn't possible to hear through the sharp ringing in his ears. He was struggling to clear his brain when another slap twisted his head to one side and he felt himself dropping through a dark pit. Blackness ebbed, threatening to take control, then he forced it to fade away. He looked through a red haze at Delano, completely ignoring Danny.

"Come on, Mr. Hern—you wouldn't want to go through that all night, would you? We'll get what we want in any case. Save yourself the pain. Make things easy."

Anger summoned the words to Greg's lips. "You can go to hell and back before I tell you a damned thing!"

There was a cold stony silence. Then Delano coughed, "Come on, my good man. You know, as well as I do, nobody can last forever. Nobody can avoid being broken. Over time, everybody breaks. Are you sure you want to play hard ball with these men? They enjoy breaking men. They would rather do that than be in bed with a woman."

Without waiting for a reply, he coldly instructed: "Okay, boys, do what's necessary."

The man turned his back.

"Stand," Danny ordered as the second goon stepped forward.

Greg didn't move.

The hand holding the gun smashed across Greg's head with such jarring impact that he was paralyzed with pain.

Blackness threatened to embrace him, but it didn't come. His mind vaguely had to admire the man for being such a professional and knowing just how hard to hit him without giving any blessed escape in unconsciousness.

Greg felt himself being lifted to his feet and his arms gripped behind him.

A fist hammered into his gut and just as he was doubling over another cut into his mouth, jerking his head back. A third blow broke at the bridge of his nose and he was aware of blood dripping down his face. He wanted to scream, but held back the impulse.

It was like swimming through a terrible river of pain, as if every nerve had been put into some horrible vice. He heard his lips moaning when something rammed at his face again. He was aware of struggling uselessly, his mind fighting for that one little focus of light which was dancing in front of his blood-filled eyes.

Then as something choked his throat with a hard

impact and he felt his legs buckle.

He wanted to pass out, to run away from the pain. Every nerve in his body screamed for them to stop, but there was still one angry part of him that held out, which refused to answer their questions and end the pain.

A dully pointed object rammed into his guts and the aim became a paralyzed knot inside his chest. He felt the world suddenly leap out from under him. It seemed as if everything had stopped. All he felt was the nausea that was bubbling in his guts and the clamp at his chest, which made all efforts to breathe useless.

It seemed like he was floating in a sea of nothingness for a long time, but it could only have been a few minutes.

A shout jarred him out of the daze. A gun exploded in his ears, ringing as if a gigantic bell had been placed over his head. Then a horror-filled scream!

His hands were released and he slumped to the floor. For a moment it seemed as if all awareness faded out and only with insane effort was he able to remain conscious enough to hear the sounds around him.

A feminine voice spoke, but the words didn't make sense to his dazed brain. He only recognized the voice.

It was Linda.

Things blurred and then he was falling again, falling downwards into the soft arms of the woman he loved. His eyes slowly fluttered open and saw, through the spinning blur surround him, the form of Linda, clutching her side, red blood ebbing between her fingers. She was leaning aback against the far wall, near the open door, a shocked white expression tormenting her lovely features.

"We have a little wild-bitch in our camp!" Delano's voice snarled.

Greg's vision was slowly clearing now. He sluggishly reached a hand toward his pocket, feeling the cold steel of the automatic. He had to get it, he had to use it against these damned bastards. His mind was on the edge of insanity, it was struggling blindly, without reason, without any logic. Only the blank madness of emotions tore at him to do something, anything.

Then his fingers clutched around the gun and he quickly brought his hand free of the pocket.

"Hold it. Don't move, anybody!" he ordered in a weak voice.

Linda's face brightened and then she managed to smile crookedly. But it remained only momentarily. Alarm froze it.

Greg started to get to his feet when something exploded at the back of his skull. There wasn't even time to think about the complete defeat that now had become his reality.

He slipped to the floor, unconscious.

* * * * * *

Coming out of the dark pit that had folded painfully around him was a long agony. The blackness ebbed and throbbed and only in the last moments did light or sound filter through the fluttering dimension in which he was trapped.

Greg couldn't think clearly, or make sense out

139

of the sounds that were now bombarding his ears. It was like being in the middle of a whirlpool with everything out of focus and distorted. All he could think of was he'd put on a good one the night before. Never had he experienced such a hangover. His head was a series of splinters, spikes driven through it in every angle.

"Okay—get up, *Agent Green!*" came a voice out of the confusion surrounding him.

That jarred awareness. Everything returned to sharp focus as if his mind had been looking through a telescope that had suddenly been adjusted so that he could see what it was aimed at.

He tensed his muscles, struggled with his eyes, trying to force them open. And all the time his mind was screaming over and over: *How'd they find out about me?*

He strained and the effort caused lancing pains to jar through him. But finally he struggled to his feet, swaying dizzily, his mind still mudded down as if a thick slime had been poured over it. Yet words came instinctively to his lips.

"What're you talking about?" He said it at a large blurry blob in front of him that had to be Delano. Hard hands gripped his arm, supporting him, not out of kindness, but out of sadistic whim.

"We have our ways, Fed-man. There's no reason to play it smart. You play things our way—and maybe you don't end up at the bottom of the ocean."

Greg started to sway dizzily but with effort kept his balance against the man supporting him. His mind was still attempting to work, function. He had to find some means to escape; some means to survive.

140

Then jarring memory brought the image of Linda as he had last seen her, propped up against the wall, white faced, blood dripping between her fingers.

He cried out her name, instinctively searching the room with blurry eyes.

She had been carried to the sofa and laid down, somebody had given her a towel for the wound, which had become crimson by now. Beyond that they'd done nothing for her.

"You have to get a doctor," Greg mumbled weakly. "You can't leave her like that." Suddenly his mind was sharp, cleared of the fog and daze. His eyes jerked toward Delano and then back to Linda.

She smiled weakly up at him. "No—it won't do any good. Why bother, anyway? I don't care what happens to me anymore."

"She's a brave, smart girl," Delano observed in what sounded like honest admiration. "She knew we don't play it sentimental. She made her choice and her mistake was turning sides. So—what'd you expect?"

"You have to do something," Greg pleaded, weakly jerking away from Danny and staggering to her side. His legs felt watery, but determination set his muscles into action and he dropped to the floor, looking into her white face. It seemed as if all the blood had already drained away.

"Why'd you come? Why?" he asked in a tortured voice.

"I had—had to....try to save you." She sounded weak, tired. "I'm sorry about...can you forgive me?"

"Don't," Greg moaned, agonized, inwardly sick. "Don't!"

He knew suddenly just how much he loved Linda. He knew it like a blade of steel had been placed into his heart to prove the pain of his love. No matter what she had done, no matter how she had betrayed him, he couldn't help himself; he couldn't stop the emotion any more than he could stop the pounding of his heart or the breathing of his lungs.

"Isn't the love scene touching?" Delano mocked. "But we don't have time. You better start talking, Hern—and fast. You don't want us batting the woman about."

Greg whipped around, glaring hatred at the man. "You wouldn't."

"Don't be childish, Mr. Hern. This isn't some game we're playing. The sooner you realize we're serious, the better it'll be for you. For the two of you."

"What do you want to know?" Greg asked in defeat. Nothing mattered now except taking the chance of saving Linda. He'd met a woman whom he would do anything for, no matter what it might cost. Except betraying his country. He had to find some way of getting her to a doctor. "I'll tell you all you need to know—if you promise you'll take care of Linda."

Delano smiled. "I don't think you're in a position to make deals. We hold all the playing cards. Everything!"

"Don't tell him a damned thing!" Linda ordered. "He'll kill us anyway."

"But you die slow, my little two-timer," Delano pointed out. "It'll be a quick death if he tells us what we want to know. Tell us what the US Government really knows about our activities."

Greg suddenly found his mind clearing of emotion, coming back to sanity. There wasn't any such thing as making a deal with men like these. They were going to be killed either way. And no matter what the price might be, he couldn't really sell out his government.

Then he thought about Linda, her courage in coming here in a vain attempt to save him, trying to make up for what she'd done. Trying to undo the damage her words had created.

That had shown something that was far above her simple act of having set him up into this trap. What might have caused her to send him here had involved things he knew nothing about; maybe threats, maybe because she believed he'd been lying to her. A woman who thought she was being used could be a dangerous, and the very fact that Linda had reconsidered revealed her to be a woman worth loving, worth fighting—or dying—for.

Greg sighed out his defeat, seemingly relaxed. His face melted into a drawn helpless look as he stood and faced the three men.

Danny was a few feet to his left, the gun in his hand pointing toward Greg, momentarily relaxed.

Delano was several yards away, to his right. There was an outside chance he might be able to get Danny between himself and the third man. Delano wasn't any particular threat, personally.

Somehow he had to risk one last attempt. He really had little to lose. Somehow he had to manage this—or be killed in the attempt. Linda wouldn't be of any use to them if he died. The worse they would do was kill her—but she might already be dying—

better a quick death than a slow one.

It was the least he could do for her.

But none of these thoughts showed on Greg's face. He had all the appearance of defeat on his features. It was an act that had to be convincing, for if he failed, there wasn't a chance; not even a small one.

"What do you want to know?"

"Who put you on to us? What information the US Government has. Everything you might know. Anything might be of help to us." Delano's words were shot at him like whiplashes. The man's eyes were coldly probing.

Greg shifted his weight, holding his breath.

Danny had his full attention on Greg's lips, as if waiting to hear what he had to say.

"I was told by a—" was as far as Greg let his dead words go. This was only a decoy, to keep their attention averted.

He leaped, using every muscle in his body in the action.

In that moment, time seemed to. freeze, becoming solid, without movement. He reached for Danny. Every nerve and energy was centered on that one action, that one effect.

A gun exploded in the background.

Danny fended with the weapon in his hands, attempting to bring it between the two of them. His eyes were wide with alarm, but his lips snarled in a twisted grin of pleasure.

Greg's hand slashed out, chopping at the other's neck. His other hand grappled frantically for the gun.

Another bullet exploded from the other man's

gun across the room.

Greg felt Danny's fingers go limp and he quickly made a wild attempt to catch the gun in mid-air as it dropped.

His fingers swooped it out of the air as he flattened to the floor. The gun pointed, without thought, without waiting or hesitation, and he automatically fired.

He squeezed the trigger again and again.

The first bullet broke into the wall near the gunman's head. The second ripped him in the stomach, exploding blood stained the white of his shirt. The third entered his chest as he slumped to the floor.

Greg hardly waited. He twisted and faced Delano.

The heavy man had been rushing toward him. Delano braked to a stop, his face went pale and sweat formed on his forehead.

"Don't try it!" Greg warned. "Just freeze where you are!"

"Watch out, Greg!" Linda's warning shout hammered at his ears.

He jerked the gun around in time to see Danny weakly reaching out for him.

Greg squeezed the trigger and Danny fell forward onto the floor.

Delano's foot caught Greg's gun hand and the weapon flew from his fingers, clattering across the floor and smashing into the far wall.

Then the Fat Man was on Greg.

It seemed as if he were fighting a bear with mountainous strength, a wild animal tearing him apart. He was already weakened by the brutal beating he'd taken. Now the huge man pressed the advantage.

Delano's beefy fist burst pain into Greg's face. Then another blow doubled him over. It was with desperate effort that he returned the attack.

Greg's hand slammed into Delano's face, cutting the bridge of the man's nose. The blow should have stopped the man, but it didn't.

Greg slammed against Delano's huge stomach and then rammed the point of his hand into his throat. This time the man staggered and Greg followed through with a rabbit punch at the nape of the neck. Delano slumped, groaned, his hands covered his face against any further blows, as gurgling sounds tortured his throat.

One last whipping action across the neck and the huge man slammed to the floor, unconscious.

Greg stepped back and then picked up the revolver, turned to Linda and said, "Are you all right?"

There was no reply.

"Linda—Linda!" Greg cried, shaking her shoulders. "God, oh, God—Linda."

But it was too late. When he realized it, Greg collapsed, burying his head against her. Sobs wanted to choke through his throat and lips, but nothing came. He lay there for a long time, unable to think of anything except the agony of his loss, the loss of the only woman that had ever managed to touch him in a real way.

How long he lay there, he would never know. Only when the final pain had subsided and he'd forced himself to face the reality of what had happened, and the fact that there wasn't anything he

146

could do about it, was he able to move.

What was left was merely a matter of cleaning up matters.

OPERATION: DOUBLE-CROSS, BY CHARLES NUETZEL

CHAPTER TWELVE

The setting was New York: Greg Hern's pent-house apartment. The lights were dim; soft music played in the background; two drinks were sitting on an end table, only half finished. The two forms on the sofa were embracing tightly. A feminine murmur sounded and then they broke away.

"Why, Greg Hern, I do believe you've changed some," a woman's voice exclaimed. She was an old friend, a woman he'd known for several years.

"How's that?" Greg questioned, taking a cigarette and lighting it.

"I don't know. Something in the way you kiss a woman. As if you—I don't know." A strange light twinkled in her dark eyes as she gazed into his.

Greg puffed on the cigarette and then looked away. For a moment he had almost believed he was looking at Linda. After three months, the memory of Linda still chilled him. But in time, it would fade enough so that he could live with it. Love had its way of mending.

For a few moments, Greg's thoughts relived the past months. After Delano had been taken by the police and Greg had explained that he'd been working for the US Government and they'd checked with the State Department, there hadn't been much trouble. Rounding up the rest of the ring had been simple enough. Jakes had quickly confessed and spilled all the information necessary to close the case. After that Greg's job had been finished and he'd seemingly disappeared from the sight of the world for several months.

Those weeks had been spent in Hong Kong, Japan and then on the Riviera. There had been long days and nights, drinking, finding momentary escape in women who happened to flutter his way. But most of it had been a frantic attempt to face the loss of Linda, to try to clear the pain from his mind. A few days before, he'd returned to Temming to settle matters on the Renton contract. As it had turned out, Renton was innocent of any involvement with the smuggling and the contract went through as planned. Carol by this time had learned to accept him as merely another man, and they had spent several nights together before his return to the States.

"Greg Hern, you haven't been listening to a word I've said!" a female voice exclaimed, a little angrily.

Greg turned to the woman, forcing a smile. "Sorry, I was thinking a little bit."

Then she smiled. "Yes—I believe you fell in love."

"What makes you think that?"

"Oh, a girl can tell. I knew something had changed you—but didn't know what." She leaned closer, her lips pursing. He kissed her gently and then reached for his drink.

"Want to tell me about it, honey?" she asked, circling her arms around his neck.

150

"Someday, when I don't hurt so much," Greg whispered in her ear, drawing the woman tighter against him. But he didn't think that time would ever come. What had happened between Linda Bedford and himself would be something he'd hold secret within him, in a special place within his mind and memory.

Greg tore his thoughts away from the past. There was the future to look forward to—future women and future assignments.

ABOUT THE AUTHOR

Charles Nuetzel was born in San Francisco in 1934, and writes:

"As long as I can remember I wanted to be a writer. It was a dream I never thought would materialize. But with the help of Forrest J Ackerman, who became my agent, I managed to finally make it into print.

"I was lucky enough not only in selling my work to publishers but also ending up packaging books for some of them, and finally becoming a 'publisher' much like those who had bought my first novels. From there it as a simple leap to editing not only a science-fiction anthology, but also a line of SF books for Powell Sci-Fi back in the 1960s. Throughout these active professional years I had the chance to design some covers and do graphic cover layouts for pocket books & magazines."

Much of his work in covers and graphics are a result of having had a father who was a professional commercial artist, and who did a number of covers for sci-fi magazines in the 1950s and later for pocket books—even for some of Mr. Nuetzel's books.

In retirement he has become involved in swing dancing, a long time lover of Big Band jazz. But more interestingly world travels have taken him (and his wife Brigitte) across the world, to Hawaii, Caribbean, Mexico, Kenya, Egypt, Peru, having a lifelong interest in ancient civilizations. His website is full of thousands of pictures taken during these trips.